TRAINING

for L♥ve

About the Author

Amanda Kabak is the author of the novels *Upended* and *The Mathematics of Change*. She has published stories in *The Massachusetts Review*, *Tahoma Literary Review*, *Sequestrum*, and other print and online periodicals. She has been awarded the *Lascaux Review* Fiction Award, *Arcturus Review's* Al-Simāk Award for Fiction, the Betty Gabehart Prize from the Kentucky Women Writer's Conference, and multiple Pushcart Prize nominations. She's lived in Boston, Chicago, and the wilds of Florida, but her home is wherever her wife, Anna, is.

TRAINING
for L♥ve

Amanda Kabak

BELLA
BOOKS
2022

Bella Books, Inc.
P.O. Box 10543
Tallahassee, FL 32302

Printed in the United States of America on acid-free paper.

First Edition - 2022

Editor: Heather Flournoy
Cover Designer: Heather Honeywell

ISBN: 978-1-64247-348-3

PUBLISHER'S NOTE

Acknowledgments

This book started with a sketch of Charlie in a gym locker room, resigned and wary and both exactly where she was meant to be but also out of place. It was supposed to be a very different story, one I've been trying to write for decades. Instead, it turned into this, which was both surprising and delightful. When I came out, I craved stories I could recognize myself in, but they weren't mainstream thirty years ago. So I satisfied myself with romances, which I could actually find. During school, I'd walk down to the main branch of the Boston Public Library the week of midterms or finals to find a few books to keep me from studying too much, thin, distilled romances that, like Charlie in that locker room, were exactly me but not at all simultaneously. They helped ease the burden of loneliness and longing when who I was was still new. They were always there in the background, percolating inside me, so it's not surprising that almost everything I write is about love in one way or another: friendship, family, marriage, even in a passion for work. I am a romantic that way despite myself.

Thank you to all who wrote those books that I devoured when I was looking for company, trying to find myself on the page. Specifically, thanks to Jessica and the crew at Bella for falling in love with Charlie and Elizabeth and giving a home to this new type of creation of mine. Shout out to Heather Flournoy for seeing what wasn't there in the book and calling it out (and loving my love affair with the subjunctive), which has made the whole story better.

As always, I wouldn't be who I am without the last twenty-plus years with Anna—if not my better half than at least more than my equal. I've promised you another Charlie book, but, remember, patience is a virtue.

Dedication

For Anna, along with everything else.

CHAPTER ONE

Kicking and Screaming

Charlie Williamson walked through the door of her apartment and leaned back against it to latch it closed. She dropped her bag to the scuffed wood floor and sighed. Her couch crooned to her, whispering sweet nothings about the softness of microfiber and fleece, of the quietly numbing effect of back-to-back-to-back episodes of *Law & Order*. Her sweatpants were just down the hall in the dark bedroom, the shades having been drawn for several days.

Her phone rang in the back pocket of her slacks, and she knew without looking at it that it was her mother. She let the call go to voice mail, but she could hear her mom's voice in her head, saying, "Charlene Josephine, I'm worried about you." Her use of Charlie's ridiculously full given name would be a joke, but the worry would be dead serious, and Charlie felt it too. This routine of couch and *Law & Order* had been going on for two straight weeks, which was not a good sign.

Melancholic was what a girlfriend in college had deemed her. "But I like it," Terri had said, pinning Charlie to her extra-long twin and trying to caress the darkness out of her. When she failed, she decided melancholy wasn't her thing, and Charlie had seen lovers come and go for similar reasons over the last decade. Her melancholia had deepened into a diagnosis of Bipolar Type 2, a fragility of mood that spun her into quiet despair and sometimes full-blown depression several times a year. She'd been on eight different medications, ending up with the old standby—sounded-scarier-than-it-was Lithium—but she'd been doing well for months before this latest backslide and had cut her dosage down to nothing.

Still, the *Law & Order* reruns were an advanced symptom of decline. Weeks ago, her workouts started to slip, and her refrigerator had grown empty while her freezer sprouted frozen lasagnas, potpies, and half gallons of store-brand ice cream. She hadn't been out with anyone from work for drinks or pub quizzes in at least a month, and she'd missed the last three rec-league games where her colleague Trevor had brought her on as a ringer. She was always a better runner than soccer player, but in a field of middle-aged middle managers, her right wing was an asset.

She was shutting everyone out and herself down, and if she didn't turn things around one way or another, her mom would show up at her door, and her concern and can-do attitude would make things worse before they got better. Charlene Josephine. What was funny about her mom using that name now was that she'd been the first one to call her Charlie and had embraced everything different and occasionally shocking about her daughter—except for those couple years before her diagnosis when she'd self-medicated with alcohol and drugs and had gotten kicked off her college soccer and track teams.

Charlie let the strength of her mother's worry—and the echo it raised in her—carry her to her bedroom, where she bypassed her pajamas in favor of a gym bag that had gotten kicked into a corner of her closet. She slung it over a shoulder and left her apartment before she could second-guess herself, trundling down a flight of stairs to the chilly April evening outside and starting in on the five blocks to the gym. Ironically, given how active she'd always been, the best defense against the offense of her depression was plenty of exercise, fresh air, and clean eating. Of course, those things were easier said than done when darkness seeped up from nowhere and bogged down her ankles, seized up her knees.

The strangest thing about depression was how physical it could be. Yes, it often paralyzed her with indecision or self-doubt, but even if she fought through toward decisiveness, her body remained dense as lead. The strong capableness she felt at other times was strangled in fifty pounds of the absolutely wrong brain chemicals, and she craved the cradling softness of bed and couch, the deep bliss of sleep.

The gym was buzzing with fluorescence even outside its double doors, and Charlie hesitated and thought that maybe this walk was enough, especially given that she was just going to have to turn around and cover the same blocks in reverse. Fresh air would pull into and out of her lungs, and wasn't that better than the conditioned atmosphere of the gym? Why was she going to the gym, anyway, when the sidewalks and paths of her neighborhood were worn familiar from miles of running?

Everything seemed to require so much volition, every decision fraught and impossible. She heard her mom's voice in her head: "You're here. Just go inside, already." She obeyed.

In the dressing room, she sat on the blond wood bench in front of an open locker and bent to untie the double-knots on her work shoes: chunky brown oxfords. She kept her eyes down while she pulled them off, seeing, in her peripheral vision, two women crossing the open aisle in front of her, one from the outside and one from the showers, wrapped in a towel, her hair turbaned in white terry cloth, and her feet bare. Charlie knew the kind of attention she garnered in locker rooms and public toilets; it ran the gamut from curiosity at its mildest, through suspicion, all the way to downright hostility.

"Charlie" wasn't just less of a mouthful than Charlene Josephine. It suited everything about her. She'd grown up a tomboy—overalls and a whining desire for short hair—matured into a serious jock, and now, well past adolescence and knee-deep into full adulthood, she was, no mistake about it, a dyke. She was tall and just this side of flat-chested. She'd won the short hair battle with her mom at an early age and had never looked back. Now she wore it buzzed short except for a blond shock at the top that she shoved over to one side or the other, depending on the day. People either thought she was in the wrong place (as if a man wouldn't notice the distinct lack of urinals in a women's bathroom) or was contagious or recruiting for the cause. Ridiculous, but true.

Regardless, when her head emerged from the old college T-shirt she kept in this gym bag, the towel woman was staring at her. Charlie looked away, pulled out shoes and socks, and busied herself putting them on. The whole time, she felt a heaviness to the air, as if the woman's gaze turned the electrons between them into something weighty and slow. Since Charlie assumed the intent behind this attention was negative, she hurried to tie her shoes, shove her work clothes and bag into the locker, and close it with a spin of the combination dial. That little burst of adrenaline propelled her onto the treadmill and into a brisk jog, her long shorts swishing around her legs.

The pounding of her stride was the opposite of calming, and the sluggish thump of her heart felt as uncomfortable as trying to come up with pithy conversation over a beer at 3 Greens by work. It was too much, too hard, too aggressively alive in the here and now given her current state. It made her a little queasy, and she felt suddenly like crying. This was a terrible idea. She would come out of this funk without such violent intervention eventually, right? A few more days or weeks on the couch, and she'd be fine.

While she cataloged the horribleness of this activity, her legs started to work through the kinks of her recent lassitude. Her stride lengthened and footfalls softened. Her mind still churned at this continued slap in the face, but her breathing settled into a strong rhythm. The word "indignity" kept floating through her mind, a mantra of revolt against this movement when all she wanted to do was be still and quiet.

Just twenty minutes, she told herself. Exercise wasn't a miracle cure for her depressive episodes, and it would only help if she did it long enough to break a sweat. Twenty minutes and she could take a long hot shower and still have time to catch a couple episodes of *Law & Order*. Twenty minutes and she could try again tomorrow, when maybe it wouldn't be quite as hard.

She made it twenty-five before slapping the stop button, letting the belt slide her to the back of the treadmill, and hopping off. The neck and lower back of her shirt were damp enough to prove her effort. She wound her way past the ellipticals and weight stations, keeping her gaze on her feet so aggressively that when she got to the locker room, she bumped into a woman exiting when she went to enter.

It was the one who'd been staring at Charlie earlier—dressed and long hair dried but still recognizable. "Sorry," Charlie mumbled and slid by her. The woman watched her pass, and Charlie was sure she was going to say something, but she just pursed her lips and turned away.

Five years before, in this very locker room, a woman just as pretty, just as primped, had caught Charlie during a lull in traffic at the lockers and dressing tables. Against the background of a lone shower running, she'd pinned Charlie with a hazel-eyed stare and said, "I've seen you not looking at me before."

Charlie had frowned. "I don't look at a lot of people."

"Why not?"

She shifted uncomfortably on the hard bench. "It tends to make them uncomfortable."

"Well, it shouldn't."

Charlie shrugged and pulled off her sweaty shirt, half in challenge, half because she was starving and wanted to get home and have dinner.

"Being looked at is flattering."

So Charlie looked. With long, straight brown hair and those light eyes, the woman had expertly applied makeup and was dressed in what Charlie thought of as a corporate uniform: slim gray skirt and a sheer, pinstriped blouse open in a deep V.

Charlie raised her eyebrow, the woman smiled, and six months later, they broke up when Charlie had a bad run of moods that no medication could quite tame.

Tonight, she shoved her work clothes in her bag and walked home, the chill outside making her sweaty shirt grow clammy and cold. At the only convenience store between the gym and her apartment, she stopped and browsed freezer cases and the snack aisle, wanting something indulgent but not knowing what. Sadness collected behind her forehead, and she ended up at the counter with three candy bars, a bag of chips, and two ice cream sandwiches. The clerk who rang her up was cheerful, saying, "Beautiful night tonight. Finally. Spring's the worst until, well, suddenly it's not, right? Are you having a good day?"

The man (Pakistani? Indian?) looked at her with a smile and palpable expectation, but Charlie couldn't find the volition to unstick her lips and answer. She grimaced, her inability to make simple conversation filling her mouth with the foul taste of regret. He shoved her treats into a plastic bag, saying, "I was just being friendly, you know."

She took the bag and escaped, angry at herself for upsetting him and angry at him for not being able to see how painful that short non-interaction had been. She devoured one of the sandwiches on the way home, fantasizing about a long, hot shower that would leave her skin red and blood boiling. She'd swaddle herself in sweatpants, crawl on the couch, and turn on the TV. But, first, a text to her mom to short-circuit any misguided heroics. *I'm…okay. Working on it. Talk soon.*

* * *

Elizabeth McIntyre's office was on the twenty-first floor of a glass-sheathed building on Dearborn Street in the heart of Chicago's Loop. From her window, she could see downtown's bustle and the lights littering nearby skyscrapers. Some evenings, she would take calls while pacing back and forth in front of the view, letting her eyes rest from her array of oversized monitors and her soul soak up the energy of the city.

Tonight, however, she stood planted behind her desk, leaned forward against her hands, glanced at her assistant, and said, "Hell, no."

Justin folded his arms, trapping a pretty red tie against his white shirt. "Hell, yes."

This attitude was exactly why he'd lasted in his position for over two years when she'd gone through previous assistants like tissue paper—and girlfriends, her best friend, Carmen, would say. "There's no way I can do another conference. It's only April, and I'm booked solid for the rest of the year."

"I have it right here, in my meticulous notes: '11:38 a.m. May 7 last year, Elizabeth makes me give a blood oath to get her on a panel at DDD Europe next year.' So that's what I did. I've already identified one conference you can skip out on, but, and I quote, 'DDD Europe will do more for our business than any other three conferences combined.'"

Elizabeth hung her head before rolling it back and forth to stretch out her neck, which was always tight. Her long, brunette hair lay heavy down her back, and when she hit an old, probably permanent kink, a shower of stars shuttled back and forth against the darkness of the inside of her eyelids. "Okay." She lifted her head. "Fine. Sign me up and book the flights."

"Maybe you can send Dennis," Justin said.

Dennis was her VP. Smart guy, capable, decent presenter. But decent wasn't good enough for DDD Europe. "Not to that."

"You say that about all the conferences."

"He's not ready."

"You reminded me to tell you to get Dennis out there more this year."

"Justin, contrary to popular belief, I don't forget everything immediately after telling it to you. I ran this firm before you came on board, and I'm perfectly capable of running it after you leave."

"I have no doubt," he said with a smile and bowed out of her office, closing the door behind him.

Elizabeth realized she was still poised vulture-like over her desk and flopped back into her expensive ergonomic chair. It wasn't just her neck that bothered her; her back was tight, and her heart had taken to revving into overdrive at random moments, like Justin adding one more thing to her already overloaded calendar. How was she supposed to run this company when she was always off promoting it? Or at least sharing knowledge at industry events, hoping that the exposure would turn into dollars. Technical consulting was a dog-eat-dog world, and her boutique firm competed with ones ten times its size. And helmed by men, who, by the nature of having a dick, had their words taken as gospel without any effort at all—forget about needing to rack up the kind of experience and success Elizabeth had managed in her fifteen years in the business.

Her heart would *not* knock it off, and its beating set off a headache, the third one this week. She didn't have to wrap her arm in a cuff to know her blood pressure was through the roof. Her doctor had warned her about it a few years ago, which was a major reason she hadn't been back since. *Slow down* were two words Carmen had put on repeat since they'd been roommates at MIT, finally finding each other after barely making it through their first year without drowning in the sea of guys in their respective majors: computer science and biology.

Carmen claimed her own lack of looks was integral to her success in research—that and the goggles and smocks she wore at her slate lab benches. Carmen wasn't bad-looking by any stretch of the imagination, with a wide face, dark eyes, and a mop of curly hair, but Elizabeth was cursed with well-composed petite features that made guys either act like patronizing assholes or dismiss her intellect in favor of ogling her breasts. She could have given herself a bad haircut or worn baggy clothes or let her own natural tendencies result in raggedly bitten fingernails, but she refused to bow to the tech industry's flagrant misogyny.

The sky still had an inviting brightness despite how late it had somehow gotten. She stood at her floor-to-ceiling windows and looked out over the cityscape of the Loop, her favorite place in the world. Instead of going to Silicon Valley or landing at one of Boston's many startups like most people in her class, she'd followed an opportunity (not to mention a girl) out here after graduation, one where she could be a big fish in a small pond and put herself truly on the line with totally new technology— not just a new way to package searching, buying, or advertising. The girl hadn't lasted, but the job had catapulted her to the bleeding edge and kept her there.

And now she was a face in the industry, representing women's ultimate capability in this male-dominated field. She bore responsibility for more than herself and her firm but also for the women that came up to her at events or networking groups or at companies she consulted for, asking advice, confiding about discrimination, expressing admiration. As a result, Elizabeth always had to have her best foot forward, be put together both physically and mentally, get everything right.

This conference would be a boon, but it was also one that required all-new material and days of prep. After so many years of long hours and draconian effort, Elizabeth watched lights wink on in the skyscrapers around her and admitted she was getting tired. This moment of weakness crashed up against the thought of her still-crammed schedule and made her chest seize up. Her vision faded, then sharpened, then faded again, and she sagged against the window, her breath squeezing out of her in a shout for Justin.

The hospital gown was a seafoam green that looked sickly against her pale, freckled skin. By the time she'd made it into this bed in Northwestern Memorial's emergency room, her symptoms had passed, and all she wanted to do was go home. She'd been rolled out of her office on a stretcher, put into an ambulance, and wailed the couple miles over here just to end up feeling almost normal and spending hours in the waiting room once they'd ruled out a heart attack and had determined she had no risk of dying while sitting in the first-come-first-served queue. Carmen had arrived a half hour in, and they had watched a movie on the wall-mounted TV before Elizabeth had been called back, put into a gown, and had her vitals taken by a pleasant enough nurse with cheekbones so sharp he could have been a model.

Carmen said, "You need to—"

"Don't."

"I'm just saying."

"You're always just saying."

"Because you're never listening."

Elizabeth rolled her head on her pillow until she was facing her best friend. Carmen had cut her dark hair in a skull-hugging style a few weeks before, and Elizabeth wondered again if it was to capture the attention of a particular guy or if she'd done it just because she'd wanted a change. She wore jeans and a pretty blue knit top that brought out her eyes. Honestly, Elizabeth wasn't sure why Carmen was still single. Her divorce had been finalized almost two years before, but she hadn't talked about anyone new since.

To divert Carmen's attention from whatever had or hadn't happened to her, Elizabeth said, "You need to start dating again."

Carmen laughed. "Do you *really* want to go there right now?"

"What do you mean?"

"One word: Sharon."

That name felt like a slap, but Elizabeth tried to hide it. "What about her?"

"Nothing, except you've spent the last decade undermining your happiness and health, doing your weird combination of pining for and competing with her at the same time."

Sharon Stackhouse was the girl she'd followed to Chicago. Their breakup had been admittedly disastrous, but Carmen was off the mark on her analysis of Elizabeth's behavior since then. "That's ridiculous."

"Believe me, I've compiled ample evidence."

"Give me a break." Sharon was brilliant to the nines, one of those cross-functional people with stellar retention who either become the president or a billionaire. Or both. It was true that in moments of weakness, she'd looked up Sharon over the years and knew she was a serial entrepreneur and twice married (and divorced) to incredibly beautiful, incredibly femme women who, Carmen would insist, didn't have two brain cells to rub together.

Because Elizabeth knew straight denial would never get Carmen off her back, she went on. "I can't help that most people are boring compared to her. If someone doesn't stimulate me mentally, you know it's a lost cause." If a relationship bored her, she got neglectful, focusing her attention on the things that lit up her neurons. She was a thought junkie, but was that so bad?

"All I'm saying is that—"

A doctor walked into her curtained area, cutting Carmen off. The woman struck Elizabeth as more than a little Nurse Ratched-esque, though that may have been the aborted conversation talking. "Ms. McIntyre, I'm Dr. Hendricks."

"Elizabeth's fine. This is my friend, Carmen, who claims I need to slow down."

"Carmen's right on the mark there. Your blood pressure is too high, and from your reported symptoms, it sounds like you had a panic attack."

Elizabeth laughed and turned to gaze at the ceiling. "Unlikely."

"Elizabeth," Carmen said.

Dr. Hendricks asked, "Have you felt that shortness of breath before? The chest pain? Problems with your vision?"

Elizabeth rolled her lips together and stayed quiet.

"Oh, Lizzie," Carmen whispered. Elizabeth hated and loved that nickname in equal measure. Lizzie the Lezzie. They'd turned it into a joke together.

"Your heart is fine. No audible murmurs or arrythmia. I'm going to order an EKG and stress test to be sure, but I suspect you mostly need to work less and exercise a little more. I can put you on medication to lower your blood pressure, but with someone so young, I'm hesitant to start you on something if we can avoid it."

"I thought there was a pill for everything."

Dr. Hendricks gave her a smile that somehow made her seem even more sinister. "Ms. McIntyre, saying you need to change your daily routine is not my way of minimizing what you've experienced. I'd say that your body is giving you a very serious warning sign, and if you don't heed it, you could easily land back here with something much, much worse. Your friend, here, is absolutely right. You need to slow down and take care of yourself."

From behind the doctor, Elizabeth could see Carmen mouthing the words, "I told you so." The thought of how insufferable Carmen was going to be was just as bad as the changes she was supposed to make once she left this hospital.

CHAPTER TWO

Off the Couch

Sometimes Charlie couldn't decide whether she had the most perfect or most ironic job possible. She worked as a product specialist for a small retailer focused on women's athletic gear that had a cult following in Chicago but still flew well under the national radar. At RRiotWear, she was part of a team that cataloged and photographed running skirts and lacy jogging bras to make them irresistible to women with more money than sense. While Charlie appreciated new running gear like anyone else who regularly pounded the pavement, she favored plain wicking T-shirts and shorts with the longest inseam possible. She wore utilitarian bras while running but otherwise didn't need them. But by now, she knew a dozen different ways to describe breathability and body-hugging fit and had grown so comfortable with the product lines and the rest of the team that she was now one of the oldest people at the company and had no plans on leaving anytime soon.

Her manager came by her desk and hovered there while Charlie finished transferring some numbers from a crowded form into a spreadsheet. "Chucky."

"Veronica." Her boss was a former tennis pro who liked to wipe the court with Charlie when she couldn't find a better partner to play with. Charlie suspected she would age to look a lot like her: lean and mildly sun-damaged with sharp collarbones under her shirt. Of course, Veronica had long, straight hair and wore just the right amount of makeup to accentuate her cheeks and eyes, so the comparison was somewhat limited.

"Spring has finally sprung, and it's two weeks to marathon training. I assume you're in?"

RRiotWear facilitated a year-round weekly running group that blossomed into guided marathon training in late May, five months out from the Chicago Marathon in October. While Charlie had participated as a group leader and trainer for the last five years, she'd been thinking of sitting things out this time. The effort of it seemed…like too much right now. Besides, she really needed new shoes, and if the reviews they'd been putting out were right, she wasn't going to like the upgrade to her favorite model. She *hated* trying to find new shoes.

"I don't know." Charlie shrugged.

"What? Come on. We need you."

"I've got a lot going on right now…" Charlie lied and then regretted it when Veronica's eyes narrowed in suspicion. "And my knees aren't what they used to be."

"Please. You're barely thirty. Who's going to take our eight-minute-mile group?"

"How about the guy in accounting? He looks fast. Besides, no one in that group needs a trainer or cheerleading. They do it for the company."

"Fine. I'll put you down for our first-timers."

"Veronica, no."

She leaned in close enough that Charlie could smell her perfume, which had faded along with the day. It was a little powdery for Charlie's taste but pleasant enough. "I'm supposed to make sure you don't isolate yourself."

"You're kidding. She called you?" Charlie knew she should've worked harder at shielding her mom from this latest depression, but she hadn't been able to rouse the energy for it. She regretted that now.

"And I can't say no to Mrs. Williamson."

"Yeah, no one can. I guess I'll be here on Saturday for the kickoff."

Veronica strode away, and Charlie snatched up her cell phone and stormed outside, dialing her mom on the way. "Mom, I just had a little chat with my boss."

"Oh, good."

"No, not good. Not good at all."

"Well, you sound better."

"Because I'm pissed. You know I hate when you butt in like that. And telling Veronica I'm having a hard time is really crossing the line." She'd hit the sidewalk by now and paced back and forth in the cool early-May air. The 156 bus wooshed past down LaSalle, air-braking right in front of her and obscuring whatever her mother was saying, which was probably for the best. "I'm an adult, Mom. I know what I'm doing."

"Have you seen Dr. Chatterbee yet?"

Charlie had been going to the same psychiatrist for six years, and by now he trusted her to know when she needed the Lithium and when her mood would stabilize on its own. "I'm trying not to go back on my meds if I can help it."

"I think you should see your doctor. You know how long it takes your medicine to kick in once you haven't taken it for a while."

"You act like I'm minutes away from offing myself." Even on LaSalle, with traffic noise and pedestrian chatter, Charlie could feel her mom's thick silence. Speaking of crossing the line. "Sorry," she said.

"You should be."

"It's okay for me to have a hard time every once in a while. Everyone has hard times."

"There's a hard time and there's…"

"I'm here at work, okay? Not home in bed." Though it had taken an hour to drag herself upright and through a shower that had felt like an affront.

"Are you exercising? Eating right?"

Charlie leaned back against the brick of the loft building she worked in. The wall was warm from the sun, and she let it seep in through her oxford shirt, toasting her back while the late afternoon air cooled her front. "I'm working on it, and right now your pressure isn't going to help."

"Oh, honey. I just worry about you. I wouldn't be a good parent if I didn't."

"Yes, as I'd know if I had kids."

"Now you're making this worse than it has to be."

She dropped her head back and gazed up the side of her building, past its large windows and four stories to the pale blue sky. "Listen, I'll tell you when it's time to worry. I promise. And it's not time to worry. In the scheme of things, I've got hay fever, not Ebola."

Charlie knew that in this long moment of quiet, her mom was biting back a half dozen things she could say, would usually say, and Charlie appreciated her restraint. "Just take care of yourself, okay? I don't know what I'd do if anything happened to you."

"Ditto, Mom. I'll keep in better touch."

When they hung up, Charlie hesitated for a long moment before she trudged back to her desk. She should tell Veronica that she'd take the eight-minute-mile group, but after a winter of inactivity, those runs would surely kick her ass and make her want to retreat in a way that would bring all of her mom's considerable parenting skills bearing down on her. She was already sleeping ten hours a night; how could she muster the energy to run fast as well? Even though the beginners, scared and determined and mostly woefully out of shape, needed enthusiasm and active coaching, which sounded as pleasant as swallowing glass, they were more her speed this spring.

* * *

Saturday mornings were typically Elizabeth's time to savor a couple cups of French press coffee brewed at her own kitchen counter and spend a leisurely few hours taking care of the more business side of her consulting firm: billable hours, marketing campaigns, requests for big-ticket travel, and the like. All winter long, she'd curled up under a blanket on her couch, the gray and brown winter-scape of the city visible from the windows of her apartment in the South Loop. Most people coveted views of Lake Michigan, but she liked her western vista of townhomes, the "L," a spray of railroad tracks, and the Dan Ryan expressway. The city's gritty industry, the harsh physicality of it was an antidote to her virtual existence.

And so, she supposed, was this stupid marathon training group Carmen was dragging her to on this Saturday morning. Elizabeth swore the doctor's cautionary instructions had hit Carmen harder than Elizabeth herself, and in the short weeks since her brief stint in the hospital, Elizabeth's phone had pinged hourly with healthy recipes, meditation tips, spa vacations, and tech detoxes. But this marathon thing had been a consistent refrain, one that wouldn't subside until Elizabeth agreed to attend some kind of training meeting on one of her precious Saturday mornings.

Carmen had maintained a tumultuous relationship with running since she'd picked it up in college to lose her freshman fifteen, slogging along the Charles River with snow in her face or the summer sun beating down. She'd run the Chicago Marathon a few times over the last decade, during years following a rough winter in the lab or her divorce. Each time, she'd joined a different charity organization and cajoled everyone she knew (more than once) to donate to whatever cause she'd chosen. But now, with Elizabeth's supposed panic attack as a spur, she'd decided to get *serious* about training to run the beast of a thing faster, and she'd found an organization that hosted a training group specifically for her goal pace—as well as one for newcomers to the sport, like Elizabeth.

Elizabeth had dated a serious runner before, one who had her own treadmill and three pairs of running shoes in rotation at any given time and who, Carmen declared damningly, ate to run instead of ran to eat. Though Jessie's legs had been mouthwateringly gorgeous, she couldn't understand Elizabeth's habit of working late even as Jessie was devout in getting in her predawn miles. Needless to say, Elizabeth harbored a somewhat dim view of serious athletes.

This waste-of-time orientation session took place at RRiotWear's River North headquarters, a quick ride on the bus from Elizabeth's apartment. A "fun run," which sounded like an oxymoron to Elizabeth, was an optional post-meeting activity, and to appease Carmen, she'd worn tights and an old pair of gym shoes she'd unearthed in her closet. She had no intention of doing any of this, especially not ultimately running an ungodly twenty-six-point-two miles, but she knew Carmen well enough to play along until the supposed panic attack was behind them.

RRiotWear's conference room opened up with sliding doors into their main office area, and the space was packed with women. The morning was cool, so most people were in tights or pants and light jackets, but those who were clearly veteran runners were in shorts or running skirts that showed off strong, lean legs. Maybe this wasn't such a bad idea, Elizabeth thought when she saw Carmen across the room and wove her way through the sea of good-looking women. The RRiotWear staff—recognizable from the gray-and-hot pink shirts they all wore—mingled with the crowd, their faces distorted with wide, healthy, catalog-worthy smiles. How long had it been since she'd had a date? Clearly too long, she thought while her gaze roamed a shapely calf here, a long neck there, and too many pert behinds to count.

Carmen grabbed her by the arm and pulled her close. "I was sure you weren't going to show up."

"You would never let me get away with that."

Before Carmen could reply, a RRiotWear woman with a thick ponytail threaded through the back of a pink cap clapped her hands. "All right, all right! Anyone not here to kick the Chicago Marathon's ass should leave now or succumb to an infectious motivation." She made a dramatic pause and glanced around as if anyone would actually get up at that point like they'd wandered into the wrong classroom in college. "For those who have been through this with RRiotWear before, feel free to zone out while I indoctrinate the newbies."

Even though Elizabeth was one of those newbies, she only half listened while scanning the group around her. Everyone wore their hair in a ponytail or a short, no-nonsense cut, and they were all nodding and smiling, focusing on the session facilitator…except for a tall woman in the back leaning against a white column, her running cap pulled low over her face, her gaze firmly on her shoes. She wore RRiotWear colors but in a boxy, long-sleeve shirt paired with plain black shorts that landed just above her knees but still exposed frankly fantastic legs. Elizabeth was a sucker for legs. The woman's arms were crossed tightly against her chest, her shoulders pulled in. Under the brim of her hat, Elizabeth could see a smooth jawline with a hint of softness and full lips.

As if the woman could feel her staring, she looked Elizabeth's way. Her face was oddly pale with dark circles under her eyes, but those eyes…even from twenty feet away, Elizabeth felt like she could lose herself in their deep brown. The woman frowned and resumed studying her neon-green running shoes as if nothing had happened, her shoulders raising and falling in a sigh Elizabeth felt in her own bones.

Carmen's sharp elbow dug into Elizabeth's ribs, and she shot her a glare. "Raise your hand," Carmen said in a hiss. "She wants to know who the first-timers are."

Elizabeth complied and listened through the rest of orientation. Afterward, she found herself in a corner of the open space with a half dozen other first-timers and the butchy woman in the cap, who blinked a few times as if she was just waking up. She ran a hand across her mouth, cleared her throat, and said, "Hey, I'm Charlie Williamson, your mentor until the race. I'm here to keep you motivated and injury free and maybe dispense some advice along the way." Her voice was husky and not nearly as high-energy as the facilitator's. She seemed…sad, which, along with her statuesque frame, made Elizabeth actually want to pay attention.

"You might hear some people say that running a marathon is ninety percent mental, and they'd be…well, wrong." The right corner of her mouth curled up, making a dimple flirt with her cheek, but the almost smile faded quickly. "Ideally, you do the proper training so you don't have to rely on mental fortitude to gut out twenty miles when you run out of steam after the first 10K. Or end up debilitated with a stress fracture or groin pull after the race. I'm not one to mince words: this is going to take work. Consistent and more than a little unrelenting. All so you have a successful and positive experience the day of the race."

Charlie went around the group, asking about their running experience and goals for the marathon. When she got to Elizabeth, their gaze met again, and it took a moment and some serious effort for Elizabeth to keep herself from drowning in Charlie's quiet, tired eyes. She said, "Honestly, my friend, Carmen, dragged me here because she thinks I'm too stressed out. I've historically only run when chased—or to catch the train." Charlie's flicker of a smile looked more like a spasm of pain than a grin, and Elizabeth quickly added, "But I'm totally type A and always finish what I start."

She wasn't sure why she suddenly got all teacher's pet, wasn't even sure why she felt herself drawn to Charlie. Butches weren't usually her thing. She tended to crave more softness, some lipstick, nicely manicured—though short—nails. Charlie's breasts barely qualified as a handful, though that was surely exacerbated by the compression bra she wore under her baggy running shirt. Being with a butch just felt so…stereotypical, which was the one thing Elizabeth avoided like the plague. Maybe Carmen was right and she'd been neglecting her social life for so long that just about any woman looked good to her. When had she last had sex? God, was it over a year already? No wonder her gaze kept sweeping over Charlie's smooth cheeks and shapely lips.

Charlie handed them each a printed schedule. "We also have this electronically if you'd rather. You can find it on our website in the community section. It's a fairly traditional couch-to-marathon plan, so you can treat it as a guideline, but it's a good one. If you're more advanced, you can make some of the shorter runs longer; if you're just starting out, you can add some walking breaks in with the running. But if you stick with me every Saturday for the scheduled long runs, I'll make sure you get across the finish line with all your toenails intact."

The group chuckled a little uneasily at that, and Charlie made a motion to slip her hands in her pockets, but her shorts didn't have any, so she crossed her arms instead. "Okay. Anyone up for an easy three miles? Conversational pace. Walking breaks by popular demand. You can leave your things here; someone will stay and keep an eye on them."

Elizabeth glanced back at Carmen like a drowning woman looking for rescue while they headed to the exit, but Carmen just gave her a finger wave that Elizabeth vowed to punish her for later. Her group filed downstairs and to the sidewalk, where Charlie set off toward the lake, walking at a brisk pace. "We'll walk to warm up until we cross Michigan."

Within minutes of entering Streeterville and starting their jog, Elizabeth was sucking wind, her heart hammering in her chest. She thought she was having another panic attack before realizing it was just that she hadn't really exercised in years. Her shoes felt like unforgiving blocks of hard rubber, and the sidewalk unreeled under her so slowly it felt like she was standing still. There was no way in hell she was going to do this for twenty-six miles in less than six months. Or ever. While she galumphed along, pulling up the rear, she could see Charlie striding easily and talking to a plump woman who took two steps for each one of Charlie's. Elizabeth felt a pang of jealously but didn't have the fortitude to push herself to the front so she could be next to their fearless leader. Besides, how badly she was struggling was too embarrassing to broadcast.

By some miracle, she made it through the three miles without a heart attack or even having to walk very much (thanks to Chicago's many traffic lights at the tail end of their route). Charlie was waiting at the entrance to RRiotWear's door, giving each of them a quick nod, a "see you in a few weeks," a "don't forget to stretch," and a "ramp up slowly." When Elizabeth got there, though, Charlie looked down and frowned. "You need to get some proper running shoes or you'll injure yourself. I have several stores I can recommend, but make sure you get someone there to watch you run so they can determine the right kind of fit and support for your gait, okay?"

This was almost as bad as Charlie seeing up close how terribly out of shape she was, so Elizabeth made a noncommittal noise, slipped by Charlie, and found Carmen in RRiotWear's sample area, holding a cute running skirt up to her hips. "Let's go." Elizabeth pulled her toward the door. "This was a terrible idea," she whispered.

"Why, because the only firm muscles you have in your body are in your fingers from all the typing you do?"

"Yeah, and if you don't stop giving me a hard time, I'll use them to pinch the nerve in your neck that'll send you into spasms." She reached toward Carmen, who ducked away. "I just don't see in whose book marathon training equates to slowing down."

"I know you. You won't sit still long enough for yoga, not even if you plunk down a lot of money for that swanky studio near you. You make so much you won't even notice any of it missing. If doing this every week keeps you from working morning, noon, and night, I won't have to wake up in the wee hours worrying about you. Just be thankful I didn't sign you up for triathlon training."

"You know I can't swim."

"Exactly." They exited the building past Charlie, who was leaning against the red brick, her face turned to the sun, her eyes closed, her mouth soft and downturned. When they were out of earshot, Carmen said, "You know what else would make you slow down—a girlfriend."

"What, her?"

Carmen's laugh was immediate and hearty. "Oh, hell, no. I know she's nowhere near your type. You need to find some nice woman who works in something totally professional but not all that taxing—no doctors or lawyers or workaholic serial entrepreneurs. Someone who will take you shoe shopping and totally be down with an afternoon at the spa."

Carmen was right, but Elizabeth took a last lingering glance at Charlie anyway. Elizabeth's romantic history wasn't particularly long and storied, but it had carried a devoted slant toward more feminine women whom people were always surprised to find out were gay and who subverted the butch/femme trope that was way too stereotypical for Elizabeth's comfort. But every once in a while, Elizabeth would find herself privately gaga over some sporty woman with a severe haircut, not an ounce of makeup, and a heavy hint of some masculine or androgynous cologne. It wasn't that she secretly wanted a man, as too many people preferred to believe. These occasional butches were attractive *because* they were women. An electric charge of sexiness underlaid the dichotomy between their more masculine dress and demeanor and the very fact of their being female. Elizabeth told herself it wasn't PC to feel like that, but though she could control a computer six ways to Sunday, her desires weren't as securely under her prodigiously strong thumb.

* * *

After the orientation session, despite the fact that Charlie wanted nothing more than to go home, she couldn't seem to muster the effort to peel herself from the sun-warmed side of their building. Before she could set herself in motion and make her way to the Red Line and ride the dozen or so rocking stops to her apartment in Andersonville, Veronica came down and said, "I know I dragged you into it this year and saddled you with the newbies, but I thought you would at least rouse some enthusiasm for that cute woman in your group."

"Which woman?"

"The brunette with the long hair who's in way over her head."

Charlie made a noncommittal grunt even though of course she knew who Veronica was talking about. When her boss turned to her with a face pinched in concern, Charlie regretted pretending she hadn't noticed the pretty woman with the terrible shoes that did nothing for her overpronation.

Veronica said, "Okay, now I'm really worried."

"You and my mom need to stop comparing notes."

"You mother is a wonderful woman."

"Yes, I know, but I only need one of her in my life."

"That girl was really cute, though, wasn't she?"

"She wasn't a girl, and cute isn't the word I'd use. Besides, you know how much I love straight women playing matchmaker." No, she wouldn't call the brunette cute. Stunning was more like it. Cheekbones for days and a wide mouth that produced a dazzling smile when she wasn't looking charmingly (and appropriately) worried. Charlie had felt the brunette watching her, but she had a long history of garnering attention for presenting the way she did. She tried to recall the woman's name, but it remained just out of her memory's reach.

"Oh, come on. It's fun, especially for us married folks. It's the ultimate vicarious experience. I saw her looking at you."

"I doubt I'm her type."

"Okay, Eeyore. Now you're just trying to get my goat. What're you doing now? Want to grab some coffee and a cinnamon roll at Yolk?"

Charlie had every intention of going home, getting on the couch, and watching a movie or three, maybe first calling her mom with a forced cheerful voice to tell her about orientation and get points for leaving the house. At the same time, she was dreading that call—not only the untruth of it but the physical effort required to inject life into her throat and vocabulary. Maybe Veronica was right. Seeing a woman like the brunette and being exhausted at the idea of making small talk and flirting was a bad sign. Maybe it was time to call Dr. Chatterbee after all.

Besides, Veronica would probably have her committed if she passed up warm cinnamon rolls, which deserved its own food group as far as Charlie was concerned. "Coffee and sugar sound great," she said. "Lead the way."

Yolk was jammed, as always, but they bypassed most of the line by sitting at the bar. A thick-walled ceramic mug full of coffee was slid in front of her practically before she'd fully sat down, and the first sip reminded her that she hadn't eaten since a sad turkey sandwich for lunch the day before. In addition to the cinnamon roll, which she shared with Veronica, she ordered an egg white omelet chock full of vegetables instead of all the other unhealthy options on the menu that were way more appealing in her depressed state.

While they tackled the warm, gooey roll that sat in a puddle of icing on a shared plate, Veronica said, "I think it's time for you to take on more responsibility at RRiotWear."

"I've told you before that I'm not going to model." Charlie winked.

"But you'd look so cute in that spaghetti-strap tank and ruffled running skirt."

"Oh, totally. You should see my prom pictures."

Veronica choked on a bite of pastry. After coughing and taking several gulps of water, she leaned in. "Are you in a dress?"

"Not just a dress. A *backless* dress. And makeup. Short hair, though, so you'd still have a chance of recognizing me."

"I'd pay good money to see that."

"Keep sweet-talking my mom, and I'm sure she'd arrange it. It's the last evidence of me in women's clothes since I went all-in when I escaped to college." And hadn't turned back even after her college career had flamed out before she'd earned her degree.

Veronica shook her head slowly back and forth, her gaze aimed just to the side of Charlie's head, clearly imagining this lauded prom picture.

"Okay, enough. I was kind of pretty, though. I would have made a good girl if I had put my mind to it."

"I don't doubt it. I'm going to have to have a serious talk with your mom. She needs to put a photo album together of the you before you became you. But, seriously. RRiotWear. You already know the business inside and out. Jennifer's been talking about promoting me and has had me on the lookout for someone to take my place. It'd be a good raise and some travel to trade shows and partners. I think you'd be great at it, and you'd get to be involved in more executive-level discussions and have a real say in the company's direction. You've always been such a champion of the community events like this training program, and you'd be able to do more of that."

"I don't know, Veronica." Charlie toyed with a broccoli floret that had escaped the edge of her omelet. "That all sounds great, but I like to keep things…more low-key."

"You mean comatose."

She sighed and put down her fork. "Stress has historically not worked out well for me."

"I'm not proposing that you suddenly become an ER doctor."

"No, just run a quarter of the company."

Veronica shifted so she mostly faced Charlie. "I've been watching you tread water for years, now. You're bright and good at what you do, and you could do more easily. I think it'd provide a sense of purpose, not stress. You'd be inheriting a great team in a stable and growing company, not some disaster that's going to make you pull out your hair—what little of it you have."

"I told you that I don't need another mother."

"Hey, I'd kill for a mom like yours instead of mine, who's intent on bullying me into giving her another grandchild, as if two aren't more than enough."

Charlie scooted her plate as far away from her as the counter would allow. "I've been wondering for years when you and Peter were going to squeeze out another one."

"Go ahead and joke, but I'm serious." She was really angry now, her hands parked on her colorful running tights. The Dragonfly series from their catalog. Her eyebrows furrowed and nostrils flared a little bit.

"I know, all right? It's just…now's not a great time. When I'm…" She glanced around the room, leaned in, and lowered her voice even though Yolk always hosted a loud din of conversation, shouted orders, and the clatter of dishes. "When I'm struggling, it's hard for me to think about major life decisions." Veronica shifted and took a breath, but Charlie cut her off. "I know. A promotion shouldn't be a major life decision, but right now it feels like it. Can I think about it? Get used to the idea?"

"Okay. Take your time. But not too long."
"I'm sure I'll be back to normal soon."

While Charlie rode the Red Line north, she thought about Dr. Chatterbee, her most unlikely but effective psychiatrist. She'd been in a particularly bad way when she'd landed in his office on a referral from her primary care doctor. He was a balding, potbellied Indian man with an accent as thick and luxurious as his eyebrows. Charlie had done talk therapy in college and for a few years after and had been prescribed some basic antidepressants by her doctor, but a persistent and sinister darkness had prompted her mom to prod her to go see someone better equipped to help. The week before her appointment, she'd barely been able to drag herself out of bed and into the shower—had, in fact, skipped the shower most days—but she walked into his office on a wave of energy, her voice bubbling along without any real volition from her.

He let her vomit out a flow of disjointed but continuous observations about her previous lassitude, her paralyzing indecision, her persistent tiredness, her repulsion at eating or drinking or talking, which was ironic, wasn't it, considering this monologue. She was desperate for him to believe how bad she'd been despite how she was acting now. In fact, she was so focused on it that she'd forgotten to wonder how he would react to her obviously male clothing, her hair, her thick-soled Fluevog wingtips.

When she'd calmed down enough to submit to a more measured mental health history and questions about her current life, she squirmed a little when he asked her about her relationship status (decidedly single), her past relationships (nothing for the last six months, a few somewhat serious girlfriends prior), her sex drive (embarrassingly nonexistent). But he nodded and wrote notes and watched her with a pleasantly neutral expression that felt both professional and yet caring in a competent way that was a massive relief.

He'd dug in to the disaster of her junior year in college, when she'd developed hamstring issues in the fall, which had put her scholarship in peril and plunged her into her first major depression. He asked about her drinking and the drugs she'd taken to get herself out of bed and onto the soccer field, the deep physicality of her depression and the way it'd been shot through with panic. Revisiting the mess she'd made of her life was torturous, especially since she'd managed to emerge from her latest depressive episode and didn't want to think about any of this at all.

For a year they'd met monthly while trying various medications in different dosages to get and keep her stable. She hated taking medicine, and he had the patience to work with her to find the minimum effective amount of whatever she was saddled with at the time. During periods of blessed normalcy, she saw him quarterly, once even letting six months go between appointments. Before recently, she'd been doing well for so long, she'd half convinced herself that she was somehow cured. But there was no cure, just daily management that was more or less successful. Now she'd fallen off a cliff without even realizing it—or at least denying it for long enough that it felt like an impossible climb back up to easy happiness. Easy anything.

Certainly not the ease and confidence required to flirt with that brunette newbie who would totally *not* be coming back to their next group run.

CHAPTER THREE

Gearing Up

Elizabeth admitted that Carmen might be right that the marathon training program was the path to improved health, but it would do nothing for her chronic lack of leisure time. Or her pocketbook. Two and a half weeks after that orientation session, she'd already dropped more than a few hundred dollars at the Fleet Feet a mile from her apartment. She was now the proud owner of new shoes, socks, bras, and a feeling equal parts excitement and dread.

She paid herself well as the owner of her consulting firm, but she still knew the value of a dollar and would shudder at the waste if this gear sat without use in her closet. At the same time, all this stuff made her feel like a poseur, and she generally avoided that at all cost, much preferring to cement herself as the expert in whatever she set out to do. It wasn't as if she'd never exercised, but she'd always been more of a gym person, putting in a half hour on an indoor bike or rowing machine while listening to the latest technical podcast to keep up on her ever-changing industry. That three-mile run had been a humbling experience, made even worse when Elizabeth compared her struggle to the group leader's effortless stride.

Even now, Elizabeth could still picture Charlie's almost smile but told herself to forget about it. First, she was way too butch. Second, Elizabeth was way too busy to start anything with anyone. Over the last ten days, she'd gone for five (short and sweet) walk/runs, and anything more was going to require some serious changes to her daily routine, which, she admitted, was the point. She was supposed to lace up her shoes and get out there again tonight, but first she had to make it through this interminable sales meeting. She couldn't quite focus on the updates everyone had and drifted along on the thought of Charlie's legs and her low, husky voice advising her to get new shoes.

Dennis broke through her reverie. "Is that all right with you?"

"Sorry, something shiny. Can you repeat that?" *Something shiny* was the standard refrain at The McIntyre Group when someone got distracted during a conversation by a text or email or chat or any of the other million notifications or animations that flooded their laptops and phones. Just like fish, their eyes and attention darted to the latest flashy thing, and concentration went out the window.

"Sending three people to the HashiCon instead of two and two to DevConnections in Vegas instead of one."

"Do we have it in the budget?"

Tyler, her VP of Sales said, "You have to spend money to make money."

"Wow, you're just begging to be put back on a commission-only salary." Elizabeth punctuated the words with a smile that got everyone to laugh like she'd hoped. "How many leads did we get from HashiCon last year, and how many of them converted?"

Tyler and Dennis presented the numbers, she approved the additional expense, and the meeting trundled along while the light in the room shifted in that devious way that indicated the onset of evening. On the large monitor in front of them, their conference schedule was depicted as different colored blocks spattered across a calendar. Her color was the deep green of their firm's logo, and there was way too much of it on the screen. For better or worse, she was the face of their company, and it was an important face—not just because it was her, necessarily, but also because it was female. When browsing any of these conference's websites or the "Our Team" pages of their competitors, one was assaulted with a sea of white men. At the conferences, her fellow women attendees rattled around in large hotel or conference-center bathrooms while the men stood in long lines for once. They always joked that that was the best part of being an overwhelming minority in the field.

Even in her firm, it could be a struggle to maintain any kind of gender parity. Sometimes they needed a particular brand of expertise and, despite deep professional networks, they couldn't find a woman or person of color with the right skills to hire and didn't have time to train someone for the job. Still, they were a veritable Benneton of diversity compared to other companies consulting at this level, and Elizabeth knew they were stronger for it. Right in this room, Tyler actually looked like the token white man in her five-person executive and sales team. Dennis and Shannon were African American, and Alan was Vietnamese, though with an incongruous Texan accent. So many of her staff lived their regular lives outside of "the box" everyone was trying to escape that she rarely had to nudge anyone to think of creative approaches to the difficult problems they were hired to solve.

Elizabeth was violently allergic to being pigeonholed. She was a mathematician and technical wizard, equally at home mounting servers in racks, diagramming solution architectures on whiteboards, and slinging low-level code. She was as queer as a three-dollar bill but was forced to come out to just about everyone to not inadvertently pass as straight. She was constantly educating people through their unconscious prejudices and biases, and she had to come across as unimpeachable in every way for her sly public service announcements and behavior corrections to not be dismissed out of hand. There was no room for failure in any of it, which was sometimes exhausting.

She eyed the splashes of forest green on the monitor again, and when they had gotten through the last item on their agenda, she said, "Actually, I have one more thing. I was asked to give one of the keynotes at the architecture and security conference in Monterey this year, so we need to add that to the schedule. And since I can't be two places at once, I need Dennis to take the panel we were invited to at that black hat conference in Orlando." Dennis appeared admirably neutral at the news, and she waited while Tyler made adjustments to the schedule. She knew she should give Dennis or Shannon a couple of her other conferences, but the words wouldn't quite come out, not even when she thought about how disappointed Carmen would be at her passing up this opportunity to lighten her load. To *slow down*.

When the meeting had wrapped up, she walked to her corner office past one of the hoteling pods, where a few of her consultants were sitting or standing at their desks, glancing back and forth between their two large monitors. She had permanent desks and offices for the folks who worked primarily out of this location, but she also kept a roster of dedicated road warriors on staff to appease the clients who insisted on having someone physically at their site instead of the virtual consulting they primarily did—to save both them and their clients the cost (not just in dollars but environmental impact) of travel.

At her desk, she pulled up the training schedule on RRiotWear's website for the hundredth time. It had officially started on Monday, and she'd already missed one workout, though it was just thirty minutes of cross-training and core strengthening. Today was supposed to be a three-mile walk/run that she'd meant to get in this morning but had ended up standing at the kitchen counter in her pajamas for an hour, drinking coffee and reviewing a client deliverable for a large project they'd been working on for months and that was a huge revenue driver for this quarter. She knew she should no longer be involved at this level of detail, but as much as she liked running things, she sometimes missed day-to-day technical tasks and still billed herself out at frankly exorbitant rates to do recovery work on projects some other consultancy had screwed up or to provide advisory or framework development for their larger coding efforts.

It was 6:15, and her stomach grumbled already, but if she didn't get the scheduled workout in today, she wouldn't do tomorrow's, and if she didn't do tomorrow's, she wouldn't go to the group run on Saturday. If she didn't go to the group run on Saturday, her expensive purchases would nag at her from her closet, Carmen would be on her like the plague...and she wouldn't see Charlie. God, even her name was butch.

Despite the avalanche of emails overflowing her inbox and the aging items on her to-do list, she closed her laptop, slipped it in her bag, and caught the bus back to the South Loop and her apartment and the three-mile route she'd mapped out along the lake for her puny but still intimidating run/walk. If she had to torture herself with exercise, there were worse places to do it. Her route extended north along the lakefront from the Field Museum up along the Monroe Street harbor and past Buckingham Fountain, which presided just on the other side of Lake Shore Drive. The full skyline stood majestic on one side of her while the lake rolled out like a blue carpet on the other. The path was full of experienced runners and bicycle commuters and several people with their dogs out for evening strolls.

Her new shoes were cushy, and the views were wonderful, but those were the highlights. Her legs were still sore from Monday evening's solo walk/run (no, she hadn't stretched after it like Charlie had commanded at orientation), her heart hammered in the running sections, and her breath was uncomfortably ragged. The plan had told her to take things slowly, to suspend expectations, but despite her other talents, those were two things Elizabeth was incapable of doing. Though she was a wreck in actual water, she'd thrown herself into the deep end from the time she was a child, swimming her way to the top of her classes, the math team, and more science fairs than she could remember. At MIT, on scholarship, she'd completed a double major in math and computer science in four years, publishing her undergraduate theses in both subjects and then disappointing everyone by going into industry—and not just industry, but business.

Everything she tried had a real potential for failure, but that just made her more determined, partly because the stakes were high. Failure would not only be a personal disappointment for her, it would be a reflection on the capability of women in her industry. She was the face of an impugned minority, and she wasn't going to let her fellow women down—even when they sometimes took issue with her lesbianism. She supposed it was the same in sports; no woman wanted to perpetuate the idea that only women who were masculine in some way (though, honestly, loving and desiring women felt incredibly feminine to Elizabeth) could succeed in male-dominated areas—like Charlie, with her shorn hair and strong jaw and heavily muscled legs. Still, Elizabeth remembered her sadness and an undeniable feminine energy that lurked under her physical strength and her kind, quiet eyes. She was most definitely a woman, and one Elizabeth couldn't quite get out of her mind.

The thought of those legs spurred her from her walk into a run again—one that she managed to keep up for the last mile back to her apartment.

* * *

Charlie had sunk into her couch after work, but she was reading, not watching *Law & Order*, which was enough of a victory for today. She ignored the fact that she'd skipped dinner and was already tempted to spend the night out here with the lights blazing and her teeth unbrushed and face unwashed. Her approach for wrangling her moods was one of quiet delicacy and low expectations. At the same time, she tried to be firm when she could, use the different tools in her self-management toolbox to short-circuit spiraling thoughts and the absolute certainty that this time the depression wouldn't lift, that pleasure would never return, that she would end up stuck here in permanent indecision and crawling fear.

It always passed—sometimes in as quickly as days, other times as long as months. But it would pass, she would feel normal again, capable and strong, if not a little shaken. All she needed to do was ride it out and try not to succumb to despair. She buried herself in a thick science fiction novel, which was the safest thing she could find at the library—nothing about love or politics or identity or loneliness, any of the many topics that would just make things worse.

Her phone rang as she neared a chapter break, and she considered ignoring it but knew from the special chime that it was her mom. "Hey," she answered in an upbeat tone that made her molars ache.

"I'm just checking in."

"You know that your worry only makes things worse." She stretched and felt her back pop, which was the most pleasurable thing that had happened all day.

"I might lay off if I knew you were going to see the doctor."

"Two weeks from tomorrow. He's on vacation and then is booked up."

"Doesn't he have someone covering for him?"

"I'm sure he does, but this isn't an emergency. I'll probably be fine by the time I see him, anyway."

Charlie's mom knew how to work silence. In the depths of her not-talking, Charlie could feel the drumming of fingernails, the tapping of a foot, the raised eyebrow of impatience. She sat up, kicking off her fleece blanket and replacing her finger with a bookmark in her paperback. She knew her voice sounded different when she was sitting or standing versus lying down, and she needed every edge she could get to convince her mom to relax.

"Listen. I'm never going to be completely stable, and you need to accept that. I'm always going to try to stay off medication as much as I can and use all my other tools to keep myself on track. I know that's not what you want to hear, but I can't help that. You have to believe that I'm not Dad."

Her mom's silence told Charlie she remained skeptical.

"I'm not Dad. Dr. Chatterbee made that clear, remember? Remember what he said to us? I'm not the paragon of sanity that you are, but I don't get his kind of highs or lows. I would never, *never* kill myself."

This time, they were both quiet. When her father was on medication, he was taciturn—shy, almost. He existed on the downside of an even keel. Charlie knew he hated it but loved that he did it for her. He always told her that. She was the most important thing, worth an unending string of overcast days because even with a haze of clouds, he could still feel the sun. She was his sun. But when she somehow wasn't enough and he went off his medication, there was no tethering him to reality. His manic episodes might drive him from home across the border to a casino where he would lose whatever savings her mom hadn't hidden away. His depression was absolute and unyielding and, ultimately, left him hanging from the rafters in their garage, a ladder kicked over beneath him.

Charlie had it easy compared to him, a fact she reminded herself of over and over again when she went off her medications and eventually swung toward darkness. She never got truly manic—the energy and verbal diarrhea she'd had in her first session with Dr. Chatterbee was about the extent of it: excited and talkative and ready to go on an hour less sleep and half the coffee. And it never lasted long before she settled in at something more normal that retained the color and life her father had been deprived of when he was drugged into balance.

"I'm not Dad," she said again, and her mom sighed.

"I know, sweetheart."

"Dr. Chatterbee trusts me to know when I need help, and I've called him. I've doubled my B12 dose and picked up a bottle of fish oil over the weekend. I have some Lithium left from last year, but I'm just not ready to start taking it again, okay? But I will if I'm still not doing well when I see him and if he doesn't have a different approach. If he trusts me, you should too."

"Dr. Chatterbee didn't lose his husband to this."

"Dr. Chatterbee is straight, so he doesn't have a husband." Charlie knew it was a bad joke the minute it escaped her mouth, and she apologized. "I'll be careful. I promise."

"I can't lose you too."

"You won't."

Her mom went on to talk about other things: the weather, movies, a new lamp she'd purchased. Charlie tried to participate, knowing that her mom thought this kind of thing helped, the tenuous tether of normal conversation. It didn't help, though, just reminded her how far from normal she was when something that should be easy wasn't at all.

When they hung up, her mom's fear had gotten under her skin, and Charlie pulled on shoes and practically fled her apartment for a walk outside. Movement and fresh air: two of the major tools in her toolbox. Outside of Clark and Ashland, her neighborhood was fairly quiet in the evenings, but there was enough foot and car traffic to distract her from her memories of her dad's funeral, of finding him, so still at the end of that bright orange extension cord he'd used. She'd been thirteen and already too consumed by confusion about her persistent crushes on other girls to worry if she'd inherit her dad's condition, but the shock of his suicide, the choked sounds of her mom's sobs at night when she thought Charlie couldn't hear made her wonder when the other shoe would drop for her. And seven years later, it had.

"Stop it," she told herself, startling someone she was passing on the sidewalk. "Just walk. Don't think."

CHAPTER FOUR

Five Miles

Saturday morning was bright but still a little brisk when Charlie got off the "L" and made her way to RRiotWear for the first official "long" run of the training. She wondered how many of the seven people that had shown up last week would return now that they knew the amount of effort it took to actually go from couch to marathon. She decided the brunette wouldn't be there and felt a pang of disappointment even through her funk, which always shook every kind of desire right out of her. But when she rounded the last corner to RRiotWear headquarters, she saw the pretty, petite woman walking toward her, coming from the opposite direction. She had on new shoes, which Charlie noticed but reminded herself that most women wouldn't pass up an opportunity to shop, given the slightest provocation. She winced at the gross generalization of that thought but couldn't stop an inward shrug. Stereotypes existed for a reason.

The brunette stood at the building's entrance and held the door for Charlie. "Thanks," Charlie said. "Nice kicks. Did you get properly fitted for those? Did they size them up from your regular shoes?"

"They measured me every which way and gave me a size that would've made me faint as a teenager, when I stopped just short of binding my feet to keep them small."

"Good. Your body will thank you." *If you keep up with it,* Charlie thought but kept to herself. She really wished her unrelenting negativity would go away, but getting tired of the darkness was actually a sign that she might be nearing the end of it. Charlie glanced over at the woman while they climbed the wide flight of stairs to RRiotWear's office. Though she carried a few extra pounds, they clung to her in all the right places, translating to curves Charlie's body didn't come close to approaching. For one thing, the brunette (what was her name?) had full breasts and wore one of those sports bras that lifted and separated them instead of squashing them into a uniboob. She felt herself staring and lifted her gaze to the woman's face to stop it. In the dim of the stairs, her eyes looked brown, but Charlie remembered them being lighter on the run last week. Maybe they were green. Or hazel? What was hazel aside from a mixed-up brown? The main character in the book she was reading had gray eyes, which always irritated her because they showed up way more in the pages of books than in real life. Had she ever even seen gray eyes? Were they just a dark hazel? Or blue? Did it depend on the light?

The woman's voice startled her. "You'll find that I never quite grew out of my teacher's pet phase. There's nothing I hate more than disappointing people."

Maybe she had oodles of teacher's-pet determination, but it was like she'd read Charlie's thoughts and responded to that challenge. Charlie had been letting people down on a somewhat regular basis since her diagnosis—including Veronica, who was still waiting on an answer about this potential promotion. "Something tells me that extends to yourself, too, right?"

One dark eyebrow raised in response. "Very astute."

"You'll need to be careful with yourself and this training. Twenty weeks is a long time, and over all those miles, something will inevitably not go according to plan. If you're too hard on yourself..." She shrugged.

"I'll keep that in mind."

Charlie couldn't be sure, but she swore the woman's tone had turned hard. See? It wasn't just marathon training that could go off the rails. She tried to shake it off while she waited for the rest of her newbie group. Miraculously, they all showed up, and they were soon walking across Michigan Avenue to run the same route they'd done at the orientation, plus an additional two miles. Most of the women admitted to adding walking breaks to their runs, so Charlie guided them in a pattern of eight-minute intervals of jogging broken up with two minutes of walking. They could complete the entire marathon this way, though Charlie had never warmed to the approach, not even when she was coming back from an injury, preferring a steady jog instead of having to lurch back and forth between those two different movements.

Despite her fairly sedentary winter, this run was ridiculously easy for Charlie. While they made their way north along the lake, waves pushed up against the concrete path in the strong breeze, and she tried to make a point of chatting with everyone in the group, dispensing clipped words of encouragement and trying to instill in them what a conversational pace felt like. Beginners almost always ran too hard too much of the time because they hadn't learned the difference between conversation versus tempo versus race paces. It was all hard to them, which was a feeling Charlie had never experienced with physical activity but knew all too well from a mental standpoint.

There were two women—Pam and Tamara—trying to lose weight after pregnancies, Wendy was getting in shape for a late-summer wedding, Denise had been dared to do it, and Jamie and Julie (Charlie was never going to be able to keep them straight) seemed to just want to meet people, which wasn't a bad reason for joining the group but might not sustain them for five months. All of these reasons could easily evaporate, but some of these women might fall in love with running and find joy in passing their time putting one foot in front of the other, watching the lake or city roll by them, feeling the afterglow of endorphins, that fabled runner's high.

She didn't end up next to the brunette (what was her name?) until their last walking break, when they'd crossed under Lake Shore Drive away from the path and into Streeterville. The home stretch, which Charlie mentioned. The brunette's cheeks were deep pink, and her eyes were green. Very green. So green Charlie didn't know how she could have forgotten.

"This is killing me," the woman said between quick breaths.

"It'll get easier."

"I'll believe it when I see it."

"It'll take a few weeks. Unless you were a smoker; then it'll take a few months."

"Thankfully, my vices are limited to coffee and whiskey. And working too much."

"This training will put a dent in your work schedule, though I know plenty of lawyers who are as addicted to marathons as they are to their billable hours."

"That's because lawyers don't need sleep. They derive all their needed energy from their insane rates."

Charlie actually smiled at that. "See? You can't be too bad off if you can still crack a joke." She checked her watch and raised her voice. "Ten more seconds and then we jog again. Last one." The group made a general groan but stayed with her when she moved out of her walk into an easy run. She led them back toward the office, walking the last several blocks while lecturing them on the importance of cooling down and stretching. Back at RRiotWear, they took over the floor of the large reception area, and she stepped them through her regular post-run stretches: quads, hamstrings, calves, hips, glutes, and IT bands. Some of the women were already highly flexible and others were clearly quite tight, including the brunette, who couldn't even come close to touching her toes.

Charlie had her change positions to try a different stretch for her hamstrings that was gentler. She got on her back next to her and demonstrated, holding her leg behind the knee and straightening it out. She turned her head to see if the brunette was paying attention, and she was somehow much closer than Charlie had thought. Looking at her from this position and at this distance was disorientingly intimate. She could see a faint spray of freckles across her nose and twin wrinkles between her eyes at her frown. Charlie cleared her throat and nodded to where she still held her own leg aloft, her shorts falling up her thigh and showing a faded tan line from her training last summer.

"Stretch enough to feel it, but it shouldn't hurt. You should be able to hold it long enough for it to actually do something, and you should be able to deepen it as you go." She waited until the brunette mimicked her to get to her feet and continue to walk around and correct people's forms—the angle of a knee here, the tilt of a hip there. "You might feel like you don't have time for this, especially as your workouts get longer, but I can pretty much guarantee that you'll get injured if you don't do it. While some of you may already be looking for a way out of this…" She paused for the few chuckles she expected and received before going on. "Injuries can linger and are always more than you bargained for. So, stretch."

After a few more minutes, Charlie declared them sufficiently loose. "See you next week. Oh, and you may think you're going to get away without any sort of lecture about food, but give me time." Who was she to talk about their eating habits when right now she cycled dizzyingly between not eating at all and narcotizing herself with sugar and fat? "Also, as much as I enjoy being at my office on the weekend, what do you guys think about meeting at the lake from now on? The other groups are doing it, and I don't like feeling left out. Where is everyone coming in from?"

They were all north-siders except one person from the Ukrainian Village and the brunette, who was in the South Loop. Those two were overridden, and they agreed to meet at the totem pole at Addison and the lake the next week, which had an adjacent parking lot and was walking distance to the Red Line stop at Wrigley Field. Charlie watched them all file out the door, though the brunette hung back, saying, "Now I get the extra challenge of going across town to torture myself, huh?"

"Majority rules. I serve at the will of the people."

"And where do you live?"

"Andersonville." Charlie smiled despite herself since that was just a couple miles from their new meeting place.

"Will of the people, my ass." But she was smiling too, and maybe standing a few inches closer than other women usually did. Wait. Was she gay? Charlie had assumed not. Given that she tended to be drawn to typically feminine love interests, most of the women she found attractive were straight. Then again, most women in general were straight. The idea that lesbians actually looked like lesbians was both outdated and still somewhat true. Charlie was a walking billboard herself.

While they gazed at each other, time slowed down a tick, and the air went thick—at least for Charlie. She'd asked straight women out before and had gotten turned down...or they'd accepted but Charlie realized they hadn't seen her invitation for coffee as anything other than friendly, which had always astounded her, given how dykey she looked. Who wouldn't doubt her intentions?

Charlie took a step back. "I'd better get going. I have a long ride back home, while I believe you're just down the street?"

"Cute. Funny. Just for that, I'll see you next week."

"If you insist," she said and watched the woman walk to the door and pull it open. "Oh, wait. What was your name, again? I'm terrible with them and have forgotten."

"Elizabeth. Elizabeth McIntyre." Charlie half expected her to wink when she said it, but she didn't and then she was gone.

* * *

Still in their running gear, Elizabeth and Carmen went for breakfast at the Dollop coffee shop near RRiotWear. Before Elizabeth could even take a sip of her Red Eye, Carmen started in. "How was the first week? Did you make all your workouts?

And aren't you supposed to be laying off the caffeine? I saw you talking with that girl Charlie. Lizzie." Her voice went low at her nickname for Elizabeth. "Were you flirting against all odds? I hope you were flirting."

Instead of answering any of those questions or the ones Carmen had lobbed at her on the two blocks over here, Elizabeth raised her mug to her lips, blew on her brew, and took a slow sip.

"Well?"

"I don't even know what question to answer, there were so many."

"I'm just excited to see you doing something other than working—or eating and drinking with me. Plus…endorphins." Carmen smiled, which made her look almost like she had at MIT—young and just happy to be where she was.

"How long until I experience this 'runner's high' firsthand? Because so far this is just kicking my ass with no measurable benefit."

"See? That's exactly the difference between software and biology. You guys expect everything right now, and we're working on top of millions of years of evolution."

"If running's that much of a long game, maybe I should try something else."

"Good thing I know what a sucker you are for a challenge. If you ever settle down with anyone, I have all sorts of tips to give her about how to manage you."

Elizabeth laughed. "As if I need to be managed."

Carmen raised her eyebrows and blinked rapidly. "Seriously?" She nodded toward Elizabeth's bag resting on the chair next to her, stuffed full and emblazoned with The McIntyre Group logo. "Says the woman who brought her laptop to a group run."

"I don't know why you're surprised. I bring my laptop everywhere. Besides, I have work to do once you're done with me."

"Once I'm—" She shook her head and waved her hand in a sharp dismissal. "Don't you have, like, a hundred people working for you?"

Closer to one-fifty now, but Elizabeth didn't volunteer that information. "They're all billable, and there's non-billable stuff to do. And, hey, I'm doing the marathon training, so maybe you can cut me some slack."

"It's just...don't you want a life? You've been working like a maniac since the first day at MIT, probably since before then, knowing you. Isn't Dennis your partner? Can't he shoulder some of the load so you can, I don't know, go out with that Charlie woman?"

"Who said I'm interested in Charlie? She's way too butch for me." But Elizabeth *had* been flirting, at least in a low-key, not-going-anywhere kind of way. The woman's legs were steel wrapped in velvet and radiated a strength that was still somehow feminine. And her smile was all that more appealing for how infrequent it was. They'd had a moment, there. Or at least Elizabeth had. But Charlie wasn't her type, was a distraction, and they probably didn't have anything in common anyway.

"Then someone else. Ms. X. The variable you *really* need to solve for."

"I'm not sure how you feel justified in riding me about this so hard when you're both divorced and single. When was the last time *you* were on a date?"

Carmen looked at her with her mouth soft and open. "Really?"

"Sorry. I'm just...you know I go on the offensive when I'm attacked."

"You run your own company in a cutthroat industry, but you can't handle a single hard truth from your best friend without lashing out?"

"I said I'm sorry."

"For your information, I went on a date last week." Carmen glanced out the window and tugged at the neck of her running shirt. "It was total shit, but that's beside the point. The point is that I *know* you're still billing hours."

Elizabeth frowned. "What can I say? People ask for me specifically, and they pay through the nose. It's good for the bottom line."

"Can't you train someone else to do what you do?"

"Some of it, sure, but…"

Carmen waited, but their sandwiches came up at the counter, and she rolled her eyes. "I'm not done with you yet," she said and got up to retrieve their breakfast.

Elizabeth started talking when Carmen sat down. "I *have* trained people. I continue to train people, but I send them out there, and they—" She shrugged and pulled off the top of her sandwich to let some steam escape so it would cool enough to wolf down. That pathetic-feeling run had really worked up an appetite. "They do all right, but they miss things. Or get bogged down in details and can't see the big picture. Or take our customers' word for things and don't ask the right questions to get at what they really need rather than what they say they want. I don't know how to teach that."

It was why she was wary of sending Dennis out in her stead—both to conferences and clients. At a big conference over a year before, he'd made an offhand remark about a technology the firm didn't have expertise in, and she'd fielded requests for it for months and had been forced to hire two expensive people to be able to meet a demand she hadn't expected them to have. Granted, it was a thriving part of their business now, but that wasn't the way to go about it. How could she trust him not to do it again and make even more work for her?

Carmen took a bite of her sandwich and waved a hand in front of her mouth while making a face at how hot it was. "God, you're such a control freak."

"I've never denied it."

"Well, you're going to control yourself into an early grave, and I'm going to be the only one at your funeral."

"Jesus, Carmen." The harshness of her best friend's words stunned her. "Way to be an asshole."

"I'm serious."

"Clearly." This exchange had caused a squeeze in her chest, and she felt her upper lip break out in a sweat she hoped Carmen wouldn't notice. She got up. "I have to pee. See? I'm hydrating."

She headed to the bathroom, trying not to look like she was hurrying, though she was.

The facilities had one of those cute gender-neutral signs: a block figure with the left half in pants and the right in a skirt, and she wondered if Charlie would appreciate that. Elizabeth wouldn't ever mistake her for a man, but she could see how other people would, which was one of the reasons they couldn't date. Elizabeth lived to subvert expectations, had made a career out of the ability, had honed subversion to an art form.

But her heart was still galloping around, and now sweat had spread to her hairline and lower back. She sat on the toilet, put her head in her hands, and breathed in for four counts and out for another four. In and out. In and out. Her vision flirted with darkness but didn't succumb, and after a few more breaths, she was able to sit up again, just a little light-headed. Maybe it was the Red Eye, and Carmen was right about caffeine. Carmen's needling didn't help, not with how it brought up her inability to drag herself out of the trenches. It wasn't as if she didn't know that had to happen. She wasn't ignorant—of business, of time management, of her own tendencies. But knowing how something *should* be and turning the heavy ship of her life was easier said than done, at least outside of the silicon-based world of computing. How was running a marathon supposed to fix that?

CHAPTER FIVE

Six Miles

Charlie sat in Dr. Chatterbee's office, which was a small, beige room that was somehow both clinical and not. Though it was on the twenty-first floor of a building not far from Northwestern Memorial, it had an uninspiring view of the building right across the street. The office sported a desk, bookcase, and two armchairs face-to-face near the window, each with its own ineffectual end table. Charlie tucked her bag between her feet and waited for Dr. Chatterbee to get himself settled with his legs crossed in just the right way, her file tucked next to his thigh, the most recent sheet from it on a clipboard balanced on a knee.

"So," he said. "Long time, no see." His voice was accented in a way that was both thick and clipped.

"Eight months. And that last one was a formality."

"Yes. You were doing well. And now?"

"The usual, again." Charlie ticked off her symptoms: lack of motivation, fatigue, loss of appetite, inability to make simple decisions. She took silly things much too hard and had cried more than once at greeting card commercials. "I'm just really fragile, and it's not getting better. Or it's getting better but really, really slowly. Nearly imperceptibly. I don't want to go back on the medicine, but…" Her gaze drifted out the window, which was still spattered with rain from that morning. She felt her mouth turn down into a frown that always preceded tears. She pressed her lips together and took in a short, fast breath through her nose.

She'd felt tired of being depressed since that first glimmer weeks before, but now her frustration with her own brain chemistry came laced through with a fear that this time her mood wouldn't be so easy to tame—not that it was ever truly easy. It had always ended up yielding, but she never quite knew whether it was because of the chemicals she dosed herself with or because her own internal ecosystem rocked its way back to a temporary equilibrium. But still being mired in depression, especially when she no longer wanted to be, brought her to a despair that kept her on the edge of tears much too often.

Dr. Chatterbee frowned. "Yes, I think it's time for us to do something. Let's talk about what you're comfortable with." Though leaving here with a prescription felt like failure, it was also a relief. She hated to think about popping pills for the rest of her life, but when she felt this stuck, taking Lithium was much easier than all the other things she and Dr. Chatterbee had tried over the years: diet and exercise, which was important no matter what, but also vitamins and omega-3s, meditation, sunlamps, spates of talk therapy and hormone balancing, not to mention varying the medication (or combination of medicines) she took as new drugs hit the market for what had become an increasingly common diagnosis.

The prescription she left Dr. Chatterbee's office with would work, eventually, but she dreaded the wait for it to kick in. And then she dreaded the semi-annual blood tests she needed to have done to make sure the medication wasn't damaging her liver or kidneys. She dreaded waiting for the prescription to be filled at the pharmacy, dreaded slipping the three pink capsules into her mouth every night, swallowing them with several gulps of water. She dreaded the tight leash she needed to keep herself on, the management and maintenance and vigilance it all required, even when she was feeling well.

She took her first dose back at the office with a swig from her stainless-steel water bottle—RRiotWear branded, of course. Veronica appeared just as she was shoving the prescription bottle into her bag, with its telltale orange plastic and bright white cap. Her boss wore a summery skirt, which contrasted starkly with Charlie's dark slacks, and Charlie thought it was time to finally put her winter clothes away and bring out the lighter colors and fabrics she wore during the warmer months. "Drinks after work tonight? The marathon crew's going to 3 Greens for beer and snacks."

She felt caught out. Alcohol was a major no-no when taking Lithium for all sorts of reasons, not even including the fact that it was a depressant, so not very helpful to her in general. If she didn't go out with them, Veronica would see it as her depression talking and give her a hard time about going home and hiding out. If she went with them and drank, especially having *just* taken a dose of her medication, she could get wonky. If she went out with them and didn't drink, she'd get gently pressed as to why. Even though they were a company invested in a fitness-oriented lifestyle (or at least looking like you had a fitness-oriented lifestyle), not raising a beer or cocktails with friends and colleagues was suspect and subject to uncomfortable conversations and stupid peer pressure.

Her indecision bloomed in her gut and tightened her throat. The smallest, easiest thing was just so *hard*, but she couldn't cry in front of Veronica, couldn't succumb to inertia and fear at the office—especially not when that idea of a promotion hung between them, charging the air.

"Uh," she said in a lame attempt to buy time and glanced down to make sure her pill bottle was out of sight. But Veronica was already looking at her strangely, and that strangeness would soon turn to something between confusion and worry (she'd seen the expression countless times on countless people—and that worry turned to anger in people she didn't know, like that convenience store clerk). If she didn't make a decision soon, Veronica might just go back to her office and call Charlie's well-meaning but meddlesome mom, which just wouldn't do.

Charlie unstuck her mouth. "Yeah, sure. Maybe for a quick burger. I've got laundry piled up to my eyeballs at home so need to take off early unless you want me going commando tomorrow." She could get a tonic water and lime when no one was looking or nurse the smallest quarter of a bottle of beer without being too conspicuous. She never drank much anyway, considering her history with the bottle back in college. She'd blacked out more times than she could count, once ending up in the emergency room with alcohol poisoning—her last strike in her tenure with the soccer team.

"Great!" Veronica did actually look excited, which warmed Charlie. "All the group leaders want to compare notes and set up some intermediate celebrations to keep people motivated. Fourth of July and Labor Day kind of things, only not right on the holidays, of course. We want to make sure we either align ourselves with Fleet Feet or CARA to coordinate water stops on the longer runs or know we're on our own and be prepared with volunteers and supplies."

"Are you bringing gear for people to try on and buy? Everyone's going to be looking for new stuff once they start getting really serious. Or they lose a few pounds, like everyone in my group seems to want to do."

"Charlie, everyone but you wants to lose a few pounds all the time."

"You don't need to lose any weight."

"You sound like my husband, that dear man. But, anyway, this is why you need to take my job. You're a natural. I know you've had time to review that position description I sent over— the one I spent way too long writing up."

She'd read it about twenty times, feeling less and less qualified the more it burned into her brain. "I need some more time to think about it."

Veronica leaned in close and lowered her voice so other people in the open area couldn't hear. "Between you and me,

Jennifer isn't going to wait very long. She's got a list of things she wants me to handle, and I can't do it until I get someone to take over my current responsibilities."

Though it was the last thing she wanted to say, Charlie felt the shameful words escape her in a whisper. "I don't have my degree."

"What do you mean?"

"I'm twenty credits short of my BA. The job description says a college degree is a requirement."

"How...we ask for a college degree for pretty much every position here, whether it actually requires one or not."

Charlie closed her eyes in a long blink. "I started part time when things were just getting off the ground, and no one ever asked. Then I just kept getting promoted little by little."

"But I know you went to college, so what happened?"

"I dropped out. I had...personal stuff to take care of."

"Huh." She stood and eased a half step back from Charlie, whether she knew what she was doing or not. Charlie had experienced the exact same thing with new friends and girlfriends over the last decade, this subconscious distancing when they found out about her lack of credentials. "I can't see how it would make a difference. You know the business intimately and have all the right skills. I mean, we're not some huge corporation that goes down a strict checklist of requirements." While she talked, Veronica seemed to have at least partly convinced herself that her words were true, but Charlie felt the lack of ease between them. "I'll run it up the flagpole and let you know what Jennifer says." Then she was gone.

Charlie sat back in her chair with a sigh. She'd held it together the first two years in college, playing soccer in the fall and running track in the spring, more of an asset than not in both sports but never a standout. But a bad breakup at the beginning of her junior year had kicked off her mood problems: prickliness, irritability, fragility, depression. She started using Adderall to get out of bed and alcohol to get to sleep, both of which eventually led to problems on the field and the track, not to mention in the classroom. That she even made it back to start her senior year was a miracle, but she hadn't even come close to finishing. She'd been meaning to pick up a class here and there and finally earn her poli-sci degree, but it was never a good time, and she'd done well enough without it. At least until now.

She reasoned that she wasn't even sure she wanted Veronica's job, but she knew she was lying to herself. And while it was good for her to want *anything* in her current state, wanting something she might not be able to have was a disaster waiting to happen.

* * *

Elizabeth was sitting on a couch in the café area of 3 Greens with a potential new hire when she saw Charlie walk in with a group from RRiotWear. In a city of millions, what were the odds? Especially since Elizabeth's office was across the river in the Loop. But one thing she'd learned was that under any big city lurked a small town—or several of them, to be accurate. Circles narrowed and converged, and the universe somehow encouraged it, like how when she learned an unfamiliar word, it suddenly appeared everywhere for a while before going back into hiding.

Elizabeth half listened to the candidate, Benjamin, and watched Charlie and her crew settle in at the bar. While this guy had a résumé chock-full of technical and consulting experience, Elizabeth had known right away that he wasn't going to fit in at The McIntyre Group. In consulting, confidence was an imperative trait to have—in spades. "Fake it until you make it" was an adage even she had lived by more than once. But there was a difference between confidence and ego, and something about this guy told Elizabeth he harbored more than just a healthy self-esteem. Still, her radar had been fooled once or twice (in both directions), and it was foolish not to at least secure a new contact in her professional network.

She tried to concentrate on Benjamin's recounting of a recovery effort he'd led at a multinational client who had poured millions into a troubled project already, but glimpses of Charlie behind him were a persistent distraction. She wore a checked work shirt with sleeves rolled up two turns, a pair of dark blue slacks, and chunky-soled shoes. Elizabeth had only seen the shorn sides and back of her head under her running cap, but the rest of her hair was honey blond and haphazardly (but attractively) pushed to the side. It made her look rakish despite the dark circles under her eyes that were clear even from across the room. Then, finally, Charlie turned to her, and their gazes met.

Zing.

It was like what she'd felt and tried to deny after the group run on Saturday. No matter how far Charlie was from her type, Elizabeth was attracted to her. Really attracted.

Benjamin had stopped talking, and Elizabeth sifted through what he'd said in order to respond. "Yes, of course. Process for the sake of process doesn't help anyone, but I know a number of consultancies that will come in and fix things but not leave the customer any way to pick up and move forward with the deliverables. We have to be as focused on mentorship as the one-off project or problem we're brought in to solve. If we don't disabuse companies—or at least groups within companies—of the cargo-cult mentality that led them to the spectacular failure in the first place, we'll also have failed in our purpose."

"That's one way to look at it." His smile was wide and toothy.

"I'm guessing you mean that's not your way. You can't have been in consulting for so long without developing your own philosophy of things, so lay it on me. If you want to be a managing partner at McIntyre, our methodologies need to at least complement each other."

Within the first few sentences, Elizabeth knew she was right about Benjamin—and that they were incompatible in more ways than too much ego. Or maybe it was all the same thing. Customers were lemmings, he said, which Elizabeth couldn't deny. Not just lemmings, but like those people trapped in Plato's cave who thought the shadows of the world they saw were reality and became so attached to that version that they violently rejected being told they were wrong.

"If people don't want to be helped out of their misconceptions, mentorship and education is impossible. And since that's ninety percent of the time, you've just got to do the best you can, take your money, and run. I mean, seriously, Elizabeth, I know you have a bunch of repeat customers that keep making the same mistakes. Otherwise you wouldn't stay in business."

She sat back and crossed her legs, her skirt landing right at the top of her knee. She hadn't worn a skirt since winter had started last November, and something about this meeting made her wish she was in slacks. "Actually, most of our repeat customers come to us with new projects in different divisions or in different technologies. Sometimes they actually just want training to make other teams as successful as the one we did the initial project for. I'm not saying you're wrong. There's an element of understanding which customers are ready for change and which aren't, but our industry is full of truly painful mistakes, and pain is one of the best motivators for putting your faith in experts and trying something unfamiliar."

"A true illustration of men are from Mars and women are from Venus." He laughed as if he actually expected her to find this funny. He was a nice-looking guy who brought in really good money based on the salary he was asking for, and maybe he had women lined up to date him, women who would laugh at an offensive joke or write off his mildly misogynistic worldview as the cost of being with someone successful. But Elizabeth wasn't one of them.

"I think it's just good business sense." Elizabeth made the concession of softening the statement and its negation of his stance with a smile.

He sighed as if truly disappointed. "I guess that means I'm not a good fit for McIntyre and will have to go work for one of your competitors. Or finally hang out my own shingle."

"Not that there aren't plenty of people on my staff I agree to disagree with, but since our approaches differ fundamentally, that's a deal breaker."

His smile belied the message she'd just given him. "Honestly, I'm kind of relieved, because I've wanted to ask you out since we sat down and couldn't if you were going to be my boss."

Not for the first time, Elizabeth felt a twinge of jealousy for lesbians like Charlie, who were obvious enough to repel such advances and who didn't have to come out over and over again—or run the risk of being assumed straight for so long that finally disclosing your proclivities felt like some kind of betrayal. "Thanks, but I'm not interested." Her lack of interest in him was so profound she didn't even feel the need to come out.

"So, it's true, then."

"What?"

"That you're gay."

She laughed before she could stop herself. She worked with enough men that she was intimate with the underlying fragility of their egos despite how egotistical they could act. "Because that's the only reason I wouldn't want to go out with you?" She uncrossed her legs and sat forward.

"I'm just saying—"

"I know exactly what you're saying. Yes, I'm gay. It's not some sort of shameful secret, and it's certainly not the only reason I don't want to date you." She paused and narrowed her eyes. "Did you even want the position? You must've known how we operate and that I wouldn't be interested in your approach. Did you accept this interview just to have the opportunity to ask me out?" To ask her out *and* waste her time, which was what really made her mad.

"No, of course not." But she could see his flush even in the dim lighting.

"Tell me, are you dismissive of our approach because you see something…feminine in it?"

"I don't like your approach because I think it's naïve and idealistic."

"And yet you still wanted to ask me out."

"Of course."

She crossed her legs again and settled back in the couch. "I think we're done here." She waited for him to take the hint, gather his things, and leave. She was *not* going to be the one to run away from this encounter. Only when he was out of sight did she lean her head in her hand, close her eyes, and sigh. What a fiasco. Carmen would be appalled. But probably cheered, at least a little. Someone had asked her out. And in a place where they served alcohol (and coffee and food), not in a hallway or conference room of another office.

Elizabeth worked with a lot of guys, was friends with a lot of guys, had no problem with a lot of guys. But, God, they could be such dicks. When she opened her eyes, thinking about getting some food to go and heading home, Charlie was looking at her. Elizabeth raised a hand and twiddled her fingers in a small wave. Charlie said something to her cohorts, pulled on her jacket, and walked in Elizabeth's general direction. For a minute, Elizabeth thought Charlie was going to bypass her and step right out the door, but she detoured and hovered at Elizabeth's elbow, which was still propped up on the couch's arm.

"Isn't this a little out of your neighborhood? Or do you work up here?" Charlie asked. Her husky voice cut through the noise of combined conversation and music.

"My office is in the Loop, so not that far."

"Ah, gotcha."

Elizabeth wanted Charlie to ask about the man she'd been with so she would have an excuse to make sure Charlie knew she was gay. Not just that, though. She found herself wanting to download that whole encounter. Though Carmen would understand better than Charlie since it was such a typical straight-girl (or straight-girl-appearing) thing, something about Charlie's quietly sad face invited Elizabeth to confide in her. Instead of succumbing to that desire, she said, "I ran this morning. In my slow, lurching way."

That got Charlie to crack one of her half smiles. "You really *are* a teacher's pet."

"I speak only the truth."

"Good for getting out there. It was kind of clammy early on, too. Probably the last cool morning of the summer, but I always think that when we're in store for one or two more. You're not truly safe until July, when you start wishing it wasn't so hot."

"Yeah, we'll get smacked with a triple-digit heat index sooner or later."

"Gotta love Chicago."

Were they really talking about the weather? Granted, it was the true Chicago pastime, but it was far from the personal conversation Elizabeth suddenly ached to have. Charlie glanced toward the door, but before she could say anything about leaving, Elizabeth blurted, "Do you guys come here often?" She cringed at how lame the question was.

"Often enough. People sometimes try to shake things up, but, yeah, it's kind of a regular place. I'm not much of a drinker, so I come mostly for the salad bar."

"But not tonight?" One of Charlie's eyebrows went up, which was a subtle gesture with her blond hair and the dim lighting. "I didn't see you eating over there."

"I...no. Not tonight."

What was going on with this woman? Where was the sadness coming from? And why wasn't Elizabeth irritated with it? Why did she feel like it was a problem she might be able to solve if she applied her considerable skills? It had to be wishful thinking triggered by this terrible meeting. "I like to interview people here." Potentially high-level people that she actually still interviewed, interviews that didn't require a computer or whiteboard for technical or logic questions. "It's neutral but pleasant territory."

"Oh, that was an interview? Did it not go well? He left kind of abruptly."

"I'm pretty sure he just took the meeting so he could ask me out."

"That's...ballsy."

"That's one word for it."

"I'm guessing you turned him down." That was the perfect segue into making sure Charlie knew she was gay, but Charlie went on before she could. "What are you interviewing for?"

Elizabeth gave her the standard elevator pitch for The McIntyre Group, which was something she'd run through so many times she didn't notice Charlie's face closing off until she was done with it. "Sorry, talking about my job tends to put people to sleep. No one can live without technology, but talking about it is an effective soporific to pretty much everyone."

"That's not it." Her smile looked pained and small. "You run the place? You must be really smart."

She laughed. "And yet I allowed myself to get lured out and waste forty-five minutes on an interview that wasn't really an interview." She wasn't the type to minimize her achievements and generally hated when other women did it, but something about Charlie's reaction made her hesitant. She was going to use the opportunity of bringing up the interview again to explain to Charlie what had happened and to come out to her, but Charlie glanced at the door and resettled her bag on her shoulder.

"That was entirely on the guy, not you. It was nice running into you, but I need to get going. See you on Saturday?"

"Yes, even though you're making me drive all the way up north."

"No one said this was going to be easy." But it came out without a smile and then Charlie was gone, leaving Elizabeth feeling like she was oh-and-two for the night.

* * *

Charlie was barely out of sight of 3 Greens when her phone rang. Veronica. She considered not answering, but Veronica was technically her boss, so she picked up.

"Was that the brunette from your newbie group?"

"It was."

"She's really pretty."

And smart, Charlie thought. "She's one of those type-A do-gooders. She just wanted to tell me she'd gotten her run in this morning."

"Sure, sure."

"I don't know what you're talking about."

"I'm talking about the woman being into you."

"I doubt she's even gay." Charlie watched herself walk past a darkened store window. She looked hunched and pathetic and straightened her shoulders at the sight.

"Gay or not, she's interested. Didn't you see how she looked at you? *Rapt*, I tell you."

"You've had too much to drink."

"Not nearly. Not yet. Come on, Charlie. You're a catch. Why wouldn't she be interested?"

"Because she's straight."

"If you say so."

Even if Elizabeth was gay, she was way out of Charlie's league. Whatever interest Veronica thought Elizabeth had would evaporate when she knew about Charlie's lack of a degree and her persistent but strategic underachieving. Still, despite how Charlie had protested, Veronica was right. There'd been something in the way Elizabeth had looked at her that had hinted at attraction, that had gotten Charlie's hopes up until she'd found out what Elizabeth did for a living. Not only a business owner but a business that was entirely dependent on Elizabeth's intelligence and credentials.

Charlie admitted that the degree of her intimidation was surely heightened by her fragile mental state, but Elizabeth would objectively be a lost cause even if Charlie was currently on solid ground, even if she was the most confident she could be, even if she was a touch manic. Elizabeth was gorgeous and composed. Her blouse and trim skirt toed the line between pure business and abject sensuality. She was put together in exactly the right way and radiated confidence.

Charlie thought about the content of those Lithium capsules mixing with her bloodstream, making their way to her brain. Even at this dose, it could be weeks before she saw improvement. That encounter with Elizabeth made her want to lose herself in TV, curl up on the couch in sweatpants and fleece, backslide in the worst way, abandon herself to the effectiveness of these drugs. But the drugs had always been only part of the solution, and even if Elizabeth wasn't in the cards for her, life went on, and she rooted around in her memories for her previous impatience with her depression and promised herself she would go to the gym when she got home.

If Elizabeth could fit in a run before her very important job, the least Charlie could do was twenty minutes on the stationary bike. Just twenty minutes. And she could even watch TV while she did it.

CHAPTER SIX

Eight Miles

Two weeks later, Charlie's depression broke overnight like a fever. She'd gone to bed achy with impatience, but she'd woken up a half hour before her alarm full of energy and with the air brighter and clearer than the day before. She was starving. She wanted eggs and mounds of toast, maybe a sausage link or two, but she settled for eating a breakfast burrito on her walk to the Red Line. She didn't even take a seat on the train, preferring to feel her legs push against the swaying of the car to keep herself upright.

She watched everyone on the ride downtown, noticing the array of attires (shorts versus suits) and moods, people frowning into their phones or talking loudly to their spouses or commuting buddies. She was so, so happy to be alive and out of the apartment, barreling down the elevated tracks to a job she liked and people she enjoyed working with. And she had the group long run tomorrow morning, so would see Elizabeth, who had turned out to be exactly the teacher's pet she'd claimed to be, showing up on time and going the distance.

That night at 3 Greens hadn't been Charlie's finest hour, but her self-esteem had buoyed with her mood. So what if she didn't have a college degree? So what if Elizabeth was fabulously brilliant? Charlie felt something catch in her throat with the thought but swallowed it down. She was going to go directly to Veronica when she got into the office and accept that promotion, and after that, she was going to talk to Elizabeth again on their run, maybe invite her for coffee or breakfast after their eight miles if Elizabeth was up to it. Even if Elizabeth wasn't gay, they could be friends, right? But that was a laughable, unrealistic thought. Charlie was never friends with women she was attracted to, and her attraction for Elizabeth had only grown despite her depression.

She acknowledged that maybe she still wasn't quite right and had swung a bit past her baseline thought patterns to something elevated and a little hyper. This only happened when her depression had been particularly long and deep, and it was both pleasant and a little frightening. Still, she was going to ride this wave of energy and confidence until it petered out and left her at a more even keel.

At RRiotWear, she strode into Veronica's office (that would soon be hers) and said, "I'll take it."

Veronica looked up from her laptop, and Charlie watched her eyes focus and those words sink in. Charlie expected to see Veronica's mouth curl into a smile or for her to give a deep nod of acknowledgment and acceptance, but instead she looked pained. "I wanted to tell you earlier this week, but we actually started an external search for the position."

"Well, call it off. I'm ready. I can beat the pants off anyone you could hire. I know this place inside and out."

"It's…you were so hesitant. And Jennifer was more surprised at your lack of degree than I thought she'd be. We're interviewing people with business or finance degrees. Even marketing. There's one candidate with an MBA."

Charlie leaned against the doorway, wanting to sag into the metal frame, but her body had too much energy to relax. "You're kidding me. Doesn't my experience count for something? My loyalty?"

"I'm not saying you're out of the running, but now you kind of have to go through the interview process with everyone else."

"Kind of, or actually?"

"There's a scoring rubric now, so…actually."

Charlie's anger was intense and huge, as huge as her relief had been upon waking, as huge as her excitement that Veronica had just squashed. It was a dangerous kind of energy that could easily explode in a way she'd regret, so she said, "I need to take a walk."

"Chucky," Veronica said, but Charlie was hoofing it out of the office, rattling down the stairs, and bursting through the door at the bottom into this beautiful summer day that now just taunted her. She stormed down the sidewalk, just this side of running, and made it to the river before she even knew it. The bridge rocked under her feet when the 156 bus barreled over it, and she clamped her mouth against a sound that wanted to tear out of her, a sound that felt like a combination of a shout and a growl that would make her look like a crazy person.

Crazy was a delicate word in its incredible coarseness. Crazy, mad, insane, imbalanced, wacko, loony, impaired. She wasn't crazy. She was just swinging toward an equilibrium she found harder to maintain than most people, though not as hard as others, like her dad. She could still remember the last time he'd plummeted from a mania into the depression that ultimately did him in. She remembered his panic, his sadness, his rage. Though she took after him, she wasn't like him. She could control herself, embraced functionality, worked at maintenance and productivity and relationships. She took walks instead of blowing up at her boss, despite being provoked.

Interviews? MBAs? How was she supposed to compete with that? Her chest still popped with anger, and she itched to move again, but she gripped the railing of the bridge and pulled in a deep breath and held it. And held it. And held it until a grayness crept into the edges of her vision. She released it in a rush, pulled out her phone, and called her mom.

"I might be a little manic," she admitted.

"How manic?"

"I'm not going to go gamble away my life savings, but I'm having a hard time standing still." Then she told her about the job and Veronica and the MBAs. "I'm just...I just...How could this happen the very minute I stop being depressed, the instant I get excited about taking on more responsibility?" She leaned back against the bridge and watched foot and car traffic pass by, men in sport coats and women in pantsuits and dresses, flowing into the Loop. She found herself looking for Elizabeth even though she wouldn't be coming from this direction.

"Maybe it's a blessing in disguise. Given everything, it might be wise to stay in a position that's more comfortable for a while. If you want to add some challenge, you could pick up a night class at Northeastern and make progress toward your degree."

Northeastern Illinois University wasn't far from Charlie's apartment and offered a ton of continuing education classes and catered to the commuter crowd, but that wasn't the point. "You're not hearing me." But Charlie could hear herself, and her voice was too strident. "Sorry," she said quietly, feeling a flush of shame. "This is going to pass. You know me. These ups are as stable as the weather here. A day or two. Maybe three. I'll be back to normal by Monday."

"That's not my point."

"I know your point. You've made your point my whole life."

"That's not fair, Charlie."

"Fair isn't even in the vicinity of any of this, for either of us, but mostly for me." She turned around and faced the river. The River Point building reflected the water in its arched bottom, and she focused on the prickle of sunlight on the water and in the windows of the building. "I just needed you to listen a little. Maybe take the sting out of this. You know, say you love me and that everything's going to be okay. Even if you don't believe it. Maybe especially if you don't believe it."

"Of course I love you. And everything's going to be okay. It will. I just worry. Why don't I plan a trip out there? I can take a long weekend. What do you think?"

Charlie thought it sounded great but knew they would tiptoe around each other between visiting museums and taking a cruise down this river and marveling at the skyscrapers. She could feel her mother's worry and wasn't yet in a position to reassure her that it was misplaced, especially not with her energy turned hot and testy and her depression still so fresh in her mind. They made plans for Fourth of July weekend. Her mom would take the train in from Michigan on Friday, and they'd have three days together.

After mundane conversation about timetables and reservations and special exhibits, Charlie felt a fragile sheen of control settle over her temper, and she texted Veronica before walking slowly back to the office. *I still want my hat in the ring. I'll prove myself to you and Jennifer.*

That's my girl, Veronica texted back.

* * *

Saturday morning, Elizabeth drove up Lake Shore Drive to the running group's meeting place, both excited and intimidated by the eight miles they were supposed to cover. She'd managed to hit at least three-quarters of her scheduled workouts, and the five-mile run she'd done on Wednesday had actually felt… good. It was strange. Her work calendar was as out of control as ever, but she'd packed her expensive running shoes and shorts and sports bra to her conference in Las Vegas and had even managed to get herself on the treadmill before the keynotes and sessions and panels.

Despite Wednesday's jaunt, she was operating on way too little sleep, and the so-called panic attacks hadn't shown any sign of abating. She'd had one after Charlie had bailed on their conversation at 3 Greens and another before a panel at the conference that had been so bad she'd sweat through her blouse and had had to wear a blazer the rest of the day to cover the stains. She'd been lying to Carmen about them and had fought with Dennis at the office where Justin could hear. She still found herself working late into the evening and all day on Sunday and taking on too many billable hours, but at least she didn't feel like a lumbering beast while huffing her way up and down the lakefront path. Small victories.

The other draw right now was Charlie. Though she clearly wasn't interested in Elizabeth, she'd be there this morning in shorts that showed off those perfect legs, squinting into the sun when she took off her glasses to make a point, correcting Elizabeth's form when she stretched, which made the uncomfortable pulling in her hamstrings and glutes bearable. In a perverse reaction to Charlie's shunning of her that night (and barely talking to her the next two group runs), Elizabeth had started to have vivid dreams in which Charlie's half smile and her legs and husky voice were the star players. Dreams where they were together—not just physically but emotionally—dreams she woke from with an ache at their ending and an ardent desire to go back to sleep and find herself in that world again.

She parked in the lot, slipped her car key into the small back pocket of her shorts, and walked to the totem pole. With the weather turned into full-bore summer, there were more people milling around by their meeting place. She'd noticed it was a popular spot for other running groups to meet, but this time there was a larger crowd—raucous with a particular energy Elizabeth knew well: a gay energy. It wasn't just the couple of rainbow handkerchiefs tied over heads or a hot pink T-shirt. It was that familiar bitchy sound of hopped-up gay men gossiping with each other and the throaty laugh of women not trying to contort themselves into something appealing to the average male. June was Pride month in Chicago, and it was heavy in the air here.

And then there was her ex, Jessica.

Elizabeth saw her first so was at least somewhat prepared for the expression of surprise and disbelief on her pretty face. "No. It can't be. Elizabeth?" Jessica looked tremendous as usual, long, dark blond hair barely restrained in a thick braid, her low-cut running shirt revealing the press of cleavage in her sports bra. They'd broken up a few years before—or Jessica had broken up with her a few years before—so at least the sting of seeing her had dulled with time.

Still, Elizabeth's smile felt sickly. "Yeah. It's been a while. Fancy meeting you here and everything."

"And everything? I can't believe you're...Are you a runner now?" She turned to the person next to her, a statuesque Black woman with hair cut tight to her fine head. "You would *not* believe how much shit this woman gave me about my running 'habit' while we were together."

Now Elizabeth's smile felt not only sickly but frozen on her face. "Yeah, well things change, Jess."

"Still working insane hours?"

"Actually, I've been cutting back," Elizabeth lied.

"How's Carmen?"

Right. By the end, Jessica had liked Carmen much more than Elizabeth. "Stirring up potions in the lab."

"Let me guess. She's the one that got you into this."

Elizabeth looked around for something to extricate herself from this situation. Just then, like a knight in shining armor, Charlie came jogging through the tunnel under Lake Shore Drive and toward them. "Oh, there's my group leader now. I should really get going."

"Charlie?" Jessica asked.

"You know her?"

"Sure, she ran with us for years. Hey, Chuck," Jessica called and waved Charlie over.

Of course. Hadn't Elizabeth just remembered that Chicago was a small town? And the virtual gay neighborhood in it was even smaller. Why wouldn't Charlie, an inveterate runner, be involved with Frontrunners, the LGBT running group of Chicago? Had Jessica dated Charlie before Elizabeth? Or, worse, after?

Charlie jogged to a stop and looked back and forth between them. "Hey, Jessie." Her grin was wider than the half smile Elizabeth had thought was her habit. "It's warm enough for you to abandon the treadmill?"

"Finally," Jessica said. She turned to the Black woman again. "This one." She cocked a thumb in Charlie's direction. "Runs outside in all weather."

"I skip the polar vortexes." Charlie ducked her head in an adorable way, but this whole encounter felt like a train wreck to Elizabeth.

"Chuck, I know for a fact you went out in the single digits. Not counting the wind chill."

"The right gear solves everything."

"If you say so," Jessica said. "Oh, I'm being rude. Chuck, this is my girlfriend, Simone. Simone, Charlie. Or Chuck. Or Chucky. Or 'Hey you.'" The two of them shook hands, and Jessica turned and indicated Elizabeth to Simone. "And this is my ex, Liz, making a rare appearance outside her office."

Elizabeth felt Charlie's gaze snap to her while she shook Simone's warm hand and felt somewhat gratified that her grip was weak. "Nice to meet you." She glanced around and saw that the RRiotWear group had fully assembled. "Charlie and I should probably get going. She's got to motivate us through eight miles today."

Jessica said, "I thought you usually worked with the experienced folks."

There was that half smile again, but Charlie answered with only a small deviation of her very serious attention on Elizabeth. "My knees needed a break."

"I hear ya. It gets a little harder every year. But you're young yet. At least younger than us. Don't work too hard, Liz."

"Oh, I won't," she said and winced inwardly. Could she really not come up with something at all clever? A zinging parting shot for the woman she'd been with for most of a year, and her hot new girlfriend? But Charlie was still watching her while they rounded the totem pole to where their group was stretching in clearly half-assed ways.

Charlie said, "You dated Jessie?"

"Years ago."

"I…" Elizabeth waited for the usual surprise that she was gay, not that Jessica looked particularly dykey outside of Pride weekend and an irrational attachment to her leather motorcycle jacket, which she justified by saying it blocked the nasty Chicago winter wind. "I can't quite imagine you two together."

Before Elizabeth could respond, Charlie made a show of greeting everyone and preparing them for the route they would take. She was practically bubbly this morning. Maybe it was the sweet air and mild weather. Or maybe she was feeling buzzed by being let in on the inside joke of Elizabeth's lesbianism? Whatever the cause, the sound of her voice was constant background through the first couple miles of their run, while they made their way south past a small harbor and a couple of junctions with the path and access roads.

The motion of running was starting to feel familiar, though not yet easy or quite comforting. But the sound of Charlie's voice was better than the music she usually ran with, and the view of her ahead (always ahead, since Elizabeth made sure it was that way) was inspiring: the firing of her calves with every step, the swish of her shorts around her thighs, the bounce of her shirt showing a trim lower back, her shaved head visible under her running cap. Even her neck was attractive—smooth and already a little tan. The competent way she strode forward was unbearably sexy, and Elizabeth wondered why she hadn't felt that for Jessica. Maybe because she hadn't enjoyed this vantage point? Or understood the pull of putting one foot in front of the other like this for fun?

One thing was sure: Elizabeth's body had finally learned how to really sweat, going way past any semblance of a dainty glow. The front of her shirt was soaked with it by the time Charlie had made the rounds of their group and fell into jogging next to her. Elizabeth noticed a sheen of wetness on Charlie's face and neck and felt a little better.

"Isn't this easy for you?" she asked between breaths that were decidedly labored. "How are you not sweating like a pig?"

Charlie laughed, and Elizabeth almost stumbled at the low, raucous sound. Had she never heard Charlie laugh before? Something was definitely different about her this morning. "I sweat at the drop of a hat. At the slightest provocation. At just the thought of exercise. Sometimes even when unloading the dishwasher, which I admittedly run only when it's crammed so full that unloading it is epic."

"Well, it's new to me."

"You're doing great. You're a natural."

Elizabeth managed just enough extra breath for a short laugh.

"I'm serious. You have good form. Maybe a little weak in your lower abs and hip flexors, but almost everyone is. Just add a bit of strengthening to your post-run stretches."

"I barely have time to run, let alone stretch."

They jogged for a minute in silence, for which Elizabeth was thankful because keeping up her minimal end of the conversation was straining her cardiovascular system. After Charlie called for them to fall into their one-minute walking break (she was weaning them from the practice), she said, "Jessie seemed to confirm my suspicion that you're a workaholic."

"In tech, a woman has to be twice as good as a man to be taken seriously." She hadn't meant to sound defensive, let alone to substantiate Charlie's claim. "I'm trying to cut back."

"It's not a criticism. I admire your drive. And the fact that you run your own company. It's impressive." She flashed that adorable half smile but glanced away and said, "Intimidating."

"See? Even when you're gay, women are stuck in this damned-if-you-do-damned-if-you-don't situation. You have to work like crazy to be successful, and then your success drives people away."

"I didn't say being intimidating is a bad thing. Don't you think the best things in life are the most challenging? The things you think you might not be able to do? Like the marathon. Would you be this committed to the training if it was just for a 10K? Or if you were only trying to keep your heart healthy?" Her watch beeped. "We're halfway through, and you're doing great," she said, then raised her voice. "Break's over." She took off ahead at a pace Elizabeth swore was faster than they'd just been running.

Charlie's words were well and good, but who wanted to be seen as the Everest of romantic achievements? She wanted to be appealing to more people than those who were looking for something to push them beyond their limits, who wanted to really *work* for it. Then again, if Charlie's half compliment meant she was the kind of woman who found Elizabeth attractive, it might not be the worst thing.

* * *

The group flopped on the ground back at the totem pole with a collective groan. Charlie walked among them, still the cheerleader, a role that had finally not felt forced this morning. "All right! Great job, everyone. *Eight* miles. Do you know how few people can do that? You might feel like you're not going to be able to do much longer than that, let alone eighteen miles longer, but you will. Next week's a little lighter to allow you to recover from this initial ramp-up, and I promise you that your legs will be ready for more after that."

She led them through their stretches, actually finding satisfaction in seeing good form in general and at their comical moans and hisses at the pull of well-worked muscles. Despite their slow pace, she felt pretty drained herself, especially after the two miles she'd run from her apartment over here. She'd really let herself go over the winter. She'd had every intention of running home after this and stretching there, but now she didn't know if she had it in her. Besides, there was the incredibly pleasant surprise of finding out Elizabeth was gay.

Her discomfort at Charlie meeting her ex had been palpable, but Charlie wasn't sure what had caused it. Sure, Jessie had gotten in some subtle digs, but most exes did something like that. Elizabeth's awkwardness had been kind of cute; it dovetailed with Charlie's continued upswing in mood and stirred up determination to actually do something about her growing attraction. She'd barely restrained herself from giving Elizabeth unequal attention during the run and digging in to her history with Jessie, but now that her official duties were over for the morning, nothing was stopping her from finding out if her interest in Elizabeth was mutual.

She really couldn't imagine Elizabeth (Liz?) together with Jessie. Not just because they were both so incredibly feminine (had it been like dating her own twin?) but because Jessie was so chill, and Elizabeth was…high-strung wasn't quite the right word. Driven, yes. Her drive radiated from her like heat from the sun, making her more than a little forbidding. If Charlie weren't riding the edge of mania, it would probably drive her away, but this morning she felt like she could conquer anything: beating out an MBA for the job she deserved and getting Elizabeth to see her as something other than a morose drill sergeant.

Charlie made sure she was next to Elizabeth when they were finished stretching. Her legs were pale but shapely. It was the first time Charlie had seen them, and they were just as she'd imagined: an extension of Elizabeth's other curves with just the shading of muscles that would surely grow more pronounced as their training continued. Charlie reached out a hand to help her up, and Elizabeth accepted. When their fingers touched, there was a spark of electricity, and their eyes met.

Zing.

Charlie almost let go but managed to tighten her grip, pulling Elizabeth to her feet with probably more force than necessary since Elizabeth took an extra hop when she was vertical.

"Do you want to get coffee? Or breakfast? You've earned a big plate of something after that run." The words came out fast with nervousness.

"If my eating keeps pace with my miles, I'll never lose the ten pounds that have accreted over the last five years."

"I think you look great." Charlie felt a flush creep up her neck.

Elizabeth glanced down at her shoes, but Charlie caught a smile in the curves of her cheek. "Thanks. Breakfast would be nice. Do you have a place in mind?"

They negotiated for a minute and agreed on one of the many brunch spots in Andersonville—a restaurant Charlie knew would have a wait for a table, which was fine with her. Though she was distractedly hungry, it would give her more time with Elizabeth. They walked to Elizabeth's car, but Charlie hesitated before getting in, noting the luxurious leather seats. She tried not to think how much this car might have cost, how successful Elizabeth was compared to her, and just swallowed hard before saying, "I'm still pretty sweaty."

"Don't worry about it. I meant to bring a towel after last weekend but forgot, so they've already been christened."

Charlie eased into the seat, as if moving more slowly would reduce the amount of sweat transfer. Instead, it just elicited a farting noise from the leather. They glanced at each other and laughed. Elizabeth mumbled something while starting the car, something that sounded like, "That's one way to defuse the tension," and Charlie's heart revved up a notch at the thought that Elizabeth felt the same charge to the air.

The car was smooth and quiet on the short ride to the restaurant, and Charlie was pretty sure she'd never been in a vehicle this nice. It's fine, she assured herself. You don't even have a car, don't need a car in the city. There's nothing to compare it to, so there's no comparison. She spent a long moment deriding herself for even feeling inadequate since one of the benefits of nontraditional relationships was not having to play by the same rules and live in roles that came with stifling expectations and stupid worries about feeling emasculated by a woman's power and money. She wasn't even a man in the first place.

But she did kind of look like one, and she tried not to let her hesitation bloom into something even bigger by thinking about Elizabeth with Jessie, the two of them so feminine while Charlie was…Charlie. Was it even possible for Elizabeth to be attracted to both of them? But they'd had a moment. Two moments. And now Elizabeth was parallel parking with impressive skill in an improbable spot less than a block from the restaurant. "Bravo," Charlie said when Elizabeth killed the engine.

"Why, thank you. I like to feel like an expert in things. Jess would call it a compulsion."

"As if she doesn't have her own compulsions. Those sweatbands she wears on her forearms?"

Elizabeth laughed. "I *hated* those."

"I gave her shit about them for years, but she'll never give them up. She calls you Liz? Is that what you like?"

"Elizabeth or Liz. Never Betsy. Sometimes Beth but not often. Carmen calls me Lizzie, but long association makes her exempt from my typical rules."

"Lizzie as in…?"

"Yep. Lizzie the Lezzie. It was part of 'taking power' in college. You know how it is; we were all idiots in college."

Charlie said, "I like Elizabeth. It suits you." She tried to make it sound definitive and popped open her door to end the conversation, not wanting to get into what a colossal mess she'd been in college.

They put their name in at the restaurant and were given a thirty-minute estimate for the wait, which wasn't even as bad as Charlie had thought (hoped). They stood in a patch of sunshine on the sidewalk, leaning against a sliver of wall between two windows. While gazing in a very determined way across the street, Elizabeth asked, "Did you and Jess ever date?"

Charlie laughed. "No way. My tits aren't nearly big enough. Have you seen who she hooks up with?" The blurt of words reminded her that she was still riding whatever small amount of mania she ever had, and the flush of embarrassment at what she'd just said and who she'd just said it to threatened to incapacitate her. "I'm…wow. I don't know…I didn't mean…I should just…"

Elizabeth laughed and put her hand on Charlie's arm, sparking that electricity again and setting up a faint tremor in Charlie's knees. "It's okay. I'm well aware of Jess's…proclivities." She looked down at her own chest, and Charlie's gaze was drawn along. Even in their sports bra, Elizabeth's breasts were full and tempting. Charlie cleared her throat and forced herself to look back at Elizabeth's face. She was smiling. "Enough about Jess," she said. "Tell me about you."

But Charlie had no desire to talk about herself. Though the tinge of manic to her energy brought along a certain confidence (whether earned or unearned, she wasn't sure), talking about herself would likely lead nowhere good, with a dead, insane father, an overprotective mother, a résumé devoid of a college degree, and her own struggles with depression. "You know most of what there is to know. I've worked at RRiotWear practically forever. I love running, and I'm a passable right wing on the soccer field. I'm actually curious about your many areas of expertise. Parallel parking. Running your own business. Crushing a man's totally reasonable desire to land a date with you."

Elizabeth laughed. It was an easy, free sound that sent chills down Charlie's neck. Coming out of her depression had awakened more than her appetite for food. Her desire was in full bloom, and she relished the opportunity to watch Elizabeth with unabashed interest while she talked. She was an enticing blend of soft and hard. Her round cheeks and curvy figure wrapped a mind and drive that was scarily sharp. Elizabeth was way smarter than Charlie was. Out of her league in every way beyond Charlie's own physical prowess. There was no reasonable way she would be interested in Charlie, but here she was, standing a few inches too close, looking at her in a way Charlie would have to be blind not to understand.

Something in how she talked about having to work against the handicap of her femaleness in her male-dominated field made Charlie think Elizabeth might understand these bouts of depression and the constant management Charlie had to apply to her own unruly brain and her fragile moods. They were both swimming upstream against prevailing forces, even though Elizabeth's was an external stupidity and Charlie's was her own brain's chemicals. Maybe Elizabeth wouldn't get scared away or grow impatient. But sitting across a table from her, taking down cheesy omelets and a shared plate of pancakes, Charlie kept the focus of the conversation squarely on Elizabeth. Only someone not in their right mind would sully a first date with their history of mental illness.

"Wait," she said and put her hand on Elizabeth's arm, stopping a fork full of egg midway between plate and lips. "You know this is a date, right? That I asked you to breakfast because I'm interested in you, not to be…I don't know…friendly and encouraging in a running mentor kind of way?" The question felt stupid and made her feel suddenly so exposed that she petered out.

"You're cute when you're flustered."

"Is that a yes?"

Elizabeth's voice dropped in both pitch and volume when she leaned forward and said, "Yes." Her eyes were green with flecks of gold that were clear in the sunlight through the large window they sat next to. They let this moment sit between them before they both took breaths and leaned back. Elizabeth ate her bite. "Do a lot of women misunderstand your intentions?"

"A surprising amount. I don't know if they're just flattered and want to try it out and then change their mind or they're just…"

"Blind?"

"I *am* pretty obvious."

"I'm actually kind of jealous. I have to constantly come out to people or they assume I'm straight. Sometimes I wish I had a steady girlfriend just so I could drop her into conversation to make the whole thing easier. But listen to me. Steady girlfriend? I sound like I'm sixteen, not a couple years away from forty."

Charlie felt her eyebrows raise despite herself.

"Oh, you didn't know I was so old?"

"You're not old. And you look great."

"Because I'm literally never outside. No sun damage. But you're still surprised. How old are you?"

She cleaved off a bite of eggs. "I'm in my thirties."

Elizabeth smiled. "What, thirty-two?"

"Thirty," Charlie admitted.

"Great. Carmen's going to accuse me of robbing the cradle."

"Does that mean you want another date?"

Elizabeth's smile faded. "I…I'm really busy."

"Right. The workaholic thing."

"I'm leaving town for a conference tomorrow night. And have a lot of client travel this month." She glanced down at her nearly empty plate. "But I…well, like I said before, I have plans to cut back."

"How about next Saturday after our run?"

Elizabeth bit her lip, which was both adorable and frightening. Was she going to end this before they even got started? Before Charlie even had a chance to kiss her? The thought was unbearable. "The conference is through Friday and out in California, so Saturday's a travel day. I was going to miss the group run but get the miles in after the flight."

"Now that's commitment."

"Teacher's pet. I told you."

"I'll run with you. Just tell me when and where." It sounded desperate, even to Charlie, and she cringed. "If you want company, that is."

"Doing the run twice in one day isn't going to be too much for you?"

"I can handle it—at least separated by that many hours."

"That sounds great, then. I'm sure I'll appreciate the distraction." Her enthusiasm seemed sincere, and Charlie relaxed a notch.

After they ate, Elizabeth tried to pay but didn't protest too hard when Charlie suggested they split the check. They strolled to Elizabeth's car, and Charlie nodded her head toward a side street. "I'm just down that way."

"Oh, right. Well, okay."

They hesitated, and Charlie took Elizabeth's hand in both of hers. She ran her thumbs over the soft skin and watched Elizabeth's face, saw her swallow. After an interminable pause, she leaned in and down, and Elizabeth stretched up to meet her. Their kiss was soft and quiet and strangely easy, but it made Charlie's breath catch and thighs ache. She was going to leave it at almost chaste but felt a gust of Elizabeth's breath against her cheek, and their mouths eased open to deepen the kiss. The touch of their tongues and the taste of Elizabeth—orange juice and the ocean, somehow—hit her in the pit of her stomach. She suppressed a groan and pulled back before things got out of hand right there on that sidewalk.

"Yowza."

Elizabeth's cheeks were pink and her eyes wide.

"Lizzie the Lezzie," Charlie said softly and smiled. "Next Saturday?"

Elizabeth nodded mutely and looked stunned, which thrilled Charlie right into another burst of energy that sent her jogging off to her apartment.

CHAPTER SEVEN

Easy Week

Elizabeth stood in an enormous conference-center bathroom, alone except for a tall woman two sinks over. There'd been a line to the men's room when she'd come in here, and she thrilled as she always did at this small reversal. The other occupant of this echoing, tiled room reminded her of Charlie, though she looked nothing like her, had shoulder-length hair and narrow shoulders and noticeable breasts. But since their kiss, Elizabeth had seen bits of Charlie in a number of women—not to mention a few men. Her smile and hands and remarkable legs had remained distinct, though, and featured prominently in Elizabeth's fantasies. Along with her lips, which had been soft and knowing. She flushed at the thought and cleared her throat, as if that would dispel both the blood from her cheeks and the thought that had spurred it on.

The tall woman glanced at her in the mirror. "Oh. You're Elizabeth McIntyre."

"Guilty," she said with a smile but felt weirdly caught out. She finished washing her hands and pulled a paper towel from a nearby dispenser. She read the woman's name tag. "Cindy. You're from Solliance?" They were a huge player in consulting—so huge that she doubted they even counted The McIntyre Group as a competitor.

"Yeah, in the development group. Duh." She rolled her eyes. "That's probably obvious from this conference. Your name comes up *a lot* in my division. Like *a lot*. A bunch of us are going to your session after lunch."

Elizabeth's heart sped up uncomfortably. "Informal corporate espionage?"

"What? No! I mean, what? No." The woman's eyes went wide, and she held her wadded up towel a few inches over the waste receptacle as if frozen in place.

Cindy's fluster should have put Elizabeth at ease, but she could feel sweat spring up on her lower back. Why? Everything was fine. She didn't need an attack. Not right now. "Just kidding. I love sharing my techniques and experiences. Ask a lot of questions in the session. I hate listening to myself speak for ninety minutes straight." She smiled, set her purse on the counter, and started rummaging through it, hoping Cindy would take the hint and leave.

"Oh, I will. Hey…maybe I can buy you a cup of coffee later and pick your brain?"

"Sure." Her voice was starting to sound funny, and she willed Cindy away. "Grab me after my talk."

"Definitely. Thanks!"

Then she was alone. She gripped the edge of the counter and tried to breathe, but her chest squeezed tight and vision got cloudy. *Not now*, she thought, but sweat gathered on her upper lip and hairline. Breathe. Breathe. Breathe. Everything's fine. Everything's going to be fine. She thought of Charlie talking to her while she ran. Complimenting her form. Telling her she was impressive, that doing hard things was important. Elizabeth didn't know why everything felt hard lately, but it wouldn't forever, would it? Same with this attack; it would pass, even though it was still on her, hot and heavy. She would breathe through it, her heartbeat would become an unconscious pulsation, and she would go up to that podium and impress Cindy.

Wrong thought. The very idea of giving her talk made her legs weak, those legs that she'd noticed growing more fit over the last weeks of running. If Charlie were here, maybe she'd take Elizabeth's hand and rub it the way she'd done after their date that had sent tendrils of electricity up her arm, through her body, and all the way to her knees. Charlie evoked more than desire in her; she exuded a calmness that felt deliciously grounding. She would coach Elizabeth through this. She would make everything okay.

At that thought, Elizabeth's chest started to loosen up, and her breath came more easily. She grabbed a handful of paper towels and hustled to the nearest stall, where she untucked her blouse from her skirt and wiped sweat from her torso and under her arms. Was this how hot flashes were going to be? She wouldn't denounce her womanhood in a million years, but sometimes the female body was a lot to take.

Why was she still having panic attacks? Wasn't the running supposed to be helping? Or giving Dennis that one conference to loosen up her calendar? She really couldn't continue on this way. What if it happened while she was in the middle of a presentation? Or a meeting with a client (and she had one tonight)? Her body was trying to tell her something, but it was speaking in an incomprehensible language. Could Charlie translate the signals from her lungs and wrists? Ankles and spleen? Had Elizabeth's intense focus on her mind made her body feel left out? Had it become ornery with neglect?

When she was dry and put together again, she threaded her way from the bathroom through the conference center and out to the bright sunshine of the day. She checked her watch and called Carmen.

"Aren't you in California?" her best friend asked.

"I kissed Charlie on Saturday."

"What?"

"And I just had another panic attack."

"Wait, what? You kissed Charlie? The butch from RRiotWear?"

"Don't call her that."

Carmen's pause had a particular characteristic to it Elizabeth could hear from two thousand miles away. It was the pause of narrowed eyes and a tilted head. It was the pause of an affected confusion.

Elizabeth said, "What?"

"I'm not sure where to start: with your panic attack, the kiss, or your wild bristling at a mere statement of fact."

Elizabeth groaned. "I don't know what's going on. With any of it. With all of it. With my life."

"Okay, now hold on a minute. We've both been in math and science long enough to know that tackling a problem as big as your life all at once is impossible."

"Gee, thanks." Under Carmen's words and the constant whir of traffic and conference attendees, Elizabeth could still hear the faint crash of waves against some shore nearby. Would watching the mesmerizing ocean help her relax?

"I mean we need to break it down into smaller parts to find something you can actually act on. Or at least something really interesting. Charlie, huh?"

"She asked me out after our run."

"Ovaries of steel."

"It probably helped that we ran into Jess, so she at least knew I was gay. Finally."

"Still."

"I like her." It felt like both an admission of guilt and incredibly freeing.

"That's not a bad thing."

"I know, but my life—"

"Your life isn't this entity that exists outside of your control like the weather. It's made up of days, which are made up of hours, which happen minute by minute, each one of which gives you the opportunity to make a decision or two."

The flow of attendees around her had slowed to a trickle, which meant the next set of sessions was getting started. "That might help if I knew what decisions I'm supposed to be making. I know things need to change, but I just don't know how."

"Kissing Charlie seems like a good first step."

"You're just looking for a vicarious thrill."

"Come on. She's sexy. I mean, have you looked at her ass?"

"Says a woman who's hopelessly straight."

"I can understand a woman's sexiness without wanting to hop in the sack with her."

"She's young. Just barely thirty," Elizabeth said.

"So what? Lizzie, I love you, I do, and if I could will myself into feeling romantic about you, all our problems would be solved." They both laughed, two thousand miles apart. "Except for your terminal case of perfectionism. If your mad brain can deduce how something's going to fail, you never, ever go down that road unless you already have five workarounds in mind."

"Occupational hazard."

"Well, life isn't code. Science isn't code. Failure's an essential ingredient."

"But, with where I am—"

Carmen cut her off. "No one can bear the imagined expectations of a whole class of people, not even you. I know you feel responsible for making the most tremendous impression of technical-minded women ever, but at some point reality has to set in. You've got to cut yourself some slack. You're so naturally put together and have so much experience that nothing's going to fall apart if you coast for a minute. Let down your guard. Sleep with someone unexpected. And then tell me all the details."

Elizabeth wanted to spill everything to Carmen but also wasn't quite sure what everything was. All she knew was that as much as she wanted to ravish Charlie, something else was there. Or maybe could be there. Or maybe Elizabeth was deluding herself because she suddenly wanted something else to be there with *someone*. When she'd sat across from Charlie, basking in her interest and warm gaze, a cosmic desire in herself had turned on like a biological alarm clock, but instead of children, she craved a connection. Love.

Instead of saying any of that, even to her oldest friend, Elizabeth dodged. "I really need to lose ten pounds."

"God, don't we all. How was the kiss?"

She sighed. "Honestly? Dreamy. Delicious. And way too short."

They talked for a few more minutes about nothing much at all. Elizabeth could feel Carmen specifically not bringing up the panic attack and was grateful. Carmen was right: Elizabeth's life couldn't be solved as one big problem, but if she tried to solve smaller pieces without a larger context, wouldn't she stay mired in this fractured feeling? Then again, maybe she was thinking too much, as usual, and right now it was enough to enjoy the memory of Charlie's lips and hands, make it through her presentation without passing out, and drop some pearls of wisdom for that eager woman, Cindy, over mediocre conference-center coffee.

She walked to the beach to see if the rhythmic waves there would bring her to a state of zen that would make the rest of this afternoon possible.

* * *

Charlie had half expected not to hear from Elizabeth about their planned run on Saturday, but she'd gotten a text in the morning saying Elizabeth was boarding her flight and could commit to a time now that she knew she wasn't going to be delayed. It made it easier not to see her at the group run and cushioned the blow of Denise dropping out—the one who'd done it on a dare. Charlie was antsy the whole day and didn't even mind the long ride down on the Red Line to Roosevelt station in the South Loop and the walk over train tracks and under Lake Shore Drive to Elizabeth's suggested meeting place in front of the steps leading up to the Field Museum. The minor mania she'd been riding when she'd asked Elizabeth to breakfast and kissed her (oh, that kiss) had petered out by the end of the weekend, and she'd achieved a degree of equilibrium, though not without some jostling through other, darker moments.

She'd hoped her heightened mood would last her through the formal interview she'd had with Veronica and Jennifer, but she'd had to fake a degree of confidence she hadn't quite felt, not with the specter of some MBA hovering among them. She'd made sure to focus on her history with the business, the initiatives she'd come up with and their successes, the ideas she'd drafted up over the weekend for increased community exposure and how that could be translated into sales, like providing merchandise for purchase at their events instead of just pointing to special web coupon codes.

They'd seemed happy enough at the end of the interview, but they were still meeting with other candidates. Charlie had seen one arrive late on Friday, overdressed in a snappy pantsuit. They'd promised not to drag things out, but she wasn't sure what that meant. How many more candidates would be traipsing through their office? How many rounds would the process go? She'd successfully avoided interviewing for years and years and now knew she'd been right in doing so. Still, that felt a little like weakness, so she reminded herself that she was qualified despite the lack of an advanced degree (okay, any degree), that she had a good history with both Jennifer and Veronica, and that even if she didn't get the promotion, she still had a job she liked at a company she believed in.

Just then she saw Elizabeth jogging toward her and watched her quick strides and strong set to her shoulders. Sure, she was slower than Charlie, but her movements were efficient and much less awkward than they'd been at that first orientation run they'd done. Elizabeth wore a cap-sleeved pink T-shirt (one of RRiotWear's, Charlie knew), and shorts that showed off the creamy skin of her legs. Bodies in motion were Charlie's thing, and Elizabeth's was something else.

"What're you looking at?" Elizabeth said with a smile, buzzed her, and continued toward the lake. "Come on. If I stop, I'll never get started again," she called over her shoulder and, not looking where she was going, almost ran into a couple with a stroller.

Charlie laughed and launched into a jog, catching up with Elizabeth when she rounded the turn to head north along the lakefront. "You're a superstar, getting out here after flying for four hours."

"If you can believe it, I actually kind of wanted to." The words were punctuated with a couple of breaths, and Charlie resolved to do most of the talking—at least during these six miles.

"Don't look now. That sounds almost like you're becoming a 'real' runner. Though saying that would get me strung up by my thumbs in the office, and they're right. Anyone who runs is a runner. But the people who want to, who find themselves craving it, are an entirely different animal."

"And you're one of those animals?"

"A lot of the time, yeah."

"Not all?"

"Sometimes I ride my couch with as much dedication as training for a marathon. I was a sloth all winter," she admitted, "so I'm getting back into shape with you guys."

"I think you have a head start. Were you an athlete in school?"

Charlie knew she meant college and was glad it wasn't a complete lie when she said, "Yeah. Soccer in the fall and track in the spring. The 5K, mostly, though I was forced into more than a few 10Ks when they needed another body. Those hurt. It all hurt."

Elizabeth glanced at her with wide eyes. "You're not supposed to tell me that."

Charlie laughed. "You're doing great. But if any of this stuff was totally easy, would it be worth doing? Or worth putting time and dedication toward? There's something compelling about difficulty. When you accomplish something that was hard, that had the possibility of failure in it, that's something real." Those words would scare Charlie's mom, and Charlie would've had a hard time believing them—let alone saying them—just a couple months ago, but if life was just protecting yourself at all cost, was that even living? Charlie reminded herself again that she wasn't her dad.

She looked at Elizabeth, who was focused on the path ahead of them but said, "You sound like Carmen but on a totally different topic."

"What's she talking about around failure?"

"Long story, and I'm busy just trying to breathe here. Go on."

From what Elizabeth had said about herself and Carmen, failure in their lives seemed improbable—or at least in their professional lives. "No matter what I said at that very first meeting of our group, all this physical stuff is actually mental—once you get to a certain level. After running three miles becomes easy, the process turns into being about improvement, and improvement means keeping it hard. It's not enough to go the distance, you need to get to the end faster than before. Ultimately, it's a losing battle, but the mental component of it is consuming. The hurt of it has a purpose, even though I guess it's an arbitrary one that might look silly from the outside. I don't know if athletes are actually weaklings with something to prove all the time or if we're just scientists with our own bodies as laboratories." Charlie was suddenly overwhelmed with embarrassment. Had she said enough that she was just talking out of her ass at this point? Would Elizabeth call her out on it? "Not that I've competed at that level in years."

"Interesting. I get it."

That emboldened her to go on. "Balance, you know? Shouldn't that be the goal? We're a part of nature, and nature's all about balance. You can't live well denying half of yourself. I mean, if you put in your miles or your reps without engaging your mind while you do it, you're literally just going through the motions. In a certain way that's okay, but you're missing out on a whole buffet of benefits."

"Like pain?" Elizabeth's question was clearly sarcastic, but the smile she gave along with it wasn't at all convincing, and Charlie realized she'd led them to a pace that was several notches too fast. She slowed it down gradually, trying to keep Elizabeth from noticing but still giving her some relief.

"Pain is a byproduct of concentration and discipline. Mostly I'm talking about alignment. Understanding yourself. Engaging in a moving meditation. Letting your eyes rest on the horizon of the lake or the green of grass and trees. Noticing the seasons and the sound of wind, the quiet when it snows. You don't get any of that on a treadmill with music blaring in your ears, like how Jessie runs." Bringing up ex-girlfriends was probably not the best idea, so Charlie changed tack. "You don't necessarily get it on runs like this where someone's blabbing at you or you're reviewing the ups and downs of your day, though that has its own purpose, I guess."

When was the last time Charlie had talked this much? Certainly before her depression, maybe when she'd let herself have more than a half a beer when out with the RRiotWear folks. They'd covered good ground while Charlie had chatted, passing the Chicago Yacht Club and making a turn onto the river path, which was busy with a few other runners and tourists meandering down the asphalt, getting in their way.

When they approached the State Street bridge, Elizabeth said, "We turn around here. Or we could just go up and catch the bus home." Her breathing was more labored than it really should have been, given how well she'd done on the eight-miler last weekend. Charlie wondered if she'd gotten enough sleep on her business trip. She wondered what the conference had been about. If there was a lot of drinking and hookups like she'd heard about at other conferences—and had experienced a little of firsthand at large meets and tournaments in college. Though that was college, where they'd all thought they were adult but were anything but.

The thought of Elizabeth hooking up with someone out there made her wince. She was way too professional for that, wasn't she? But hadn't Charlie been imagining her in very unprofessional situations all week since that kiss? Hair spread across a pillow, eyes closed, head tilted back, exposing the pale, thin skin of her throat. The thought made Charlie's gut squeeze in a not-unpleasant way. To dispel the image, since it literally threatened to trip her up, she said, "Some days on this plan are going to be harder than others."

Elizabeth shot her a look that said, as clear as day, "Duh."

"I guess I just mean you shouldn't worry about it. There are lots of reasons for it, and it's okay for it just to suck for a little bit or even to skip a day or two if you're feeling exceptionally tired. I used to overthink the ebb and flow of it and cause myself a stupid amount of stress."

"This sucks," Elizabeth said.

"Do you want to take a walking break? I totally forgot that you usually do."

"No. If I stop, we'll be walking the rest of the way. Just keep talking to me."

As much as Charlie wanted this to be easy for Elizabeth— or at least not as unpleasant as it seemed to be today—hearing that instruction thrilled her. "Sometimes, when I want to quit, I think about how happy I'll be when I finish what I set out to do and how bad I'd feel about myself if I gave up. Sometimes it's all about the satisfaction of the end and not the run itself."

"Is it *ever* about the run?"

"Eventually, yeah. Or at least the run as a backdrop to being outside, unplugged, experiencing the turn of the hours and seasons, the different colors of the lake."

Elizabeth huffed out a breath that sounded like an aborted laugh. "I can't believe you can be poetic while you run."

"It's the only time, believe me. It's like how drinking loosens some people up."

"Well, keep going. I like it."

She told Elizabeth about the group run that morning, about the two hot days she'd missed while out in California. She talked about RRiotWear's new line of tights that, she supposed, most buyers would actually wear while grocery shopping or getting their morning coffee. She talked about focusing on one muscle group or another to keep from dwelling on an area of fatigue. If it was her quads that were screaming, put attention on the firing of her calves, on the push-off in her toes. It would slightly alter her gait and relieve the tiredness. Or at least make her feel less tired. Or suffer less with her tiredness.

"Or, I guess you could just listen to me babble."

They'd made it back to the Field Museum, where Charlie thought they were going to stop, but Elizabeth took a right, and Charlie veered off along with her. They jogged under Lake Shore Drive and up a short incline to Roosevelt Ave. Elizabeth dodged cars across the busy street, and they made their way down a quieter side street that ran parallel to Lake Shore. After a couple blocks, she finally stopped in front of an unassuming red brick building, clearly a warehouse that had been converted to lofts, like many others in the South Loop.

Elizabeth sat on some concrete steps and put her head in her hands.

Charlie said, "So much for cooling down."

Elizabeth looked up. "Bite me."

Charlie raised an eyebrow.

"You know what I mean. God, that was torture."

"But you did it."

"But I did it." Her smile was small but definitely there. She straightened a leg and made a show of stretching out her hamstring.

Charlie felt a sudden suffocating nervousness and walked to the edge of the building and back. "You're probably exhausted after your trip."

"Have dinner with me?"

Charlie glanced down at her sweaty shirt and shorts.

"Upstairs? You came all this way."

"You don't owe me anything. It was my pleasure. Happy to help and all that." Why was she talking? Or talking without just saying yes yes yes?

Elizabeth looked up at her. The sun was behind her building, so her face was shrouded in shadow, but Charlie could still somehow tell that Elizabeth was having nothing to do with the stupid "aw shucks" show she'd just put on for no good reason. Her hands searched her hips for some pockets to slip into, but these shorts only had a zippered one in the back that held her train pass, a key to her apartment, and her credit card. While she was trying not to feel like a fool, Elizabeth got up and stood on the bottom step, which put her a couple inches taller than Charlie. Then, before she knew what was happening, they were kissing again.

But this wasn't like kissing at that parking meter, sweet and soft, exploring with a quiet, agreed "yes." No, this was a meeting of their mouths with more depth and energy than Elizabeth had shown on that whole run. Charlie could still feel the plushness of Elizabeth's lips under their aggressive pressure, but then her tongue was in Charlie's mouth, and a sound part-whimper and part-groan escaped her throat. She pulled Elizabeth to her, her hands finding the damp back of her T-shirt, the flare of her hips. It was as if all of Charlie's nerve endings migrated to her lips and tongue. Even her teeth. She was awash in a desire more urgent than she'd felt in a long time—if ever.

They only pulled apart when they heard the door behind them open with a metal clang of its push bar. "Uh," Charlie said. Slick.

Elizabeth nodded toward the door. "Come on."

She followed Elizabeth but felt suddenly shy. All that talking she'd done during their run, and she'd successfully said next to nothing about herself, especially about the parts of her that Elizabeth might not like very much. They stood on opposite sides of the elevator during its slow ride up to the sixth floor—the penthouse. Of course. Elizabeth's eyes were smoldering, the green darker in the dim elevator, her eyelids heavy with desire, and Charlie suddenly wished for a twelve-week training plan for this. Instead of couch-to-marathon, couch-to-bedroom. It had been over a year since her last girlfriend, and that relationship had barely qualified as one, petering out only a few months in. Their sex had started out hot and new, but had almost immediately become rote and infrequent—a change Charlie had blamed on the Lithium she'd been on at the time, but didn't it take two to tango?

Thinking about an ex-girlfriend and sexual inadequacy was the last thing she should be doing right at this moment. The elevator groaned to a halt, and Elizabeth took her hand to guide her down the hall to a plain wood door at the end. She fished out a key from her shorts, opened it, and pulled Charlie inside. They were kissing again before Charlie could even get a look at the place, but it was short this time because Elizabeth said, "I need a shower."

"I—"

Charlie's hesitation wasn't in the script Elizabeth was using, and she blinked a few times as if processing it. "Oh."

"No, I just—"

"I thought—"

"No, I do. I just—"

Elizabeth put a hand to her face and looked away. "I'm so—"

"No, you're not."

"I'll just—"

Charlie took Elizabeth by the arms to stop this fruitless exchange. "Why don't you take a shower, and I'll make us dinner."

"Oh. So, you don't want to leave?"

Charlie smiled. "No. But I do want to eat."

Elizabeth's gaze skittered away from Charlie again. "There's nothing in the house."

"Nothing? I doubt that. I'm a miracle worker with odds and ends."

"I've…been out of town for a week. Why don't we just order in? I have a whole drawer of menus."

Charlie took Elizabeth's hand and liberated the keys from her fingers. "I'll run to the grocery. Literally. You'll still be in the shower when I get back. Any dietary restrictions I need to know about?"

Elizabeth laughed. "At this point, I'll eat anything that's not nailed down."

"I'll be back in a jiffy." Charlie eased her way out of the apartment. She took the stairs and, true to her word, ran the few blocks to a store she'd spotted before the run. She blitzed through the aisles, picking up lettuce, cucumber, fennel, tomato, scallion, some ridiculously expensive salad dressing, salmon, eggs, and crusty bread. She considered wine but remembered her medicine and decided against it with a pinch of regret. She ran back to the apartment, paper bag cradled and crinkling in her arms. The shower was still on when she let herself in.

"I'm back," she said loudly. "Take your time. Dinner in thirty minutes."

"Okay."

Elizabeth's apartment wasn't at all ostentatious, but it was… really nice. Huge windows faced south and west, letting in the rosy orange of the slowly setting sun. The ceilings were ridiculously high, planks of wood crossed by enormous, square beams. The walls were the same red brick as the building's exterior, studded with sconces that shone with a soft, warm light. The kitchen reposed in a corner of the main area, shiny and modern and outfitted to the nines. It was clearly a selling point of the place, but when she opened the refrigerator and some cabinets, it was equally as clear that Elizabeth never cooked. The emptiness Charlie found spoke of much more than a week out of town. In fact, the whole apartment felt a little…forlorn. Neglected. At least they weren't at Charlie's place, which was probably a quarter of the size and hadn't yet been cleaned of months of depressive accumulation. How much money did Elizabeth make?

To distract herself from that question, Charlie washed her hands and face in the kitchen sink, then, throwing caution to the wind, pulled off her top and ducked her head under the warm spray to rinse salty sweat residue from her hair. She splashed water on her torso and arms and patted dry with a paper towel. She hung her shirt over the back of a stool pulled up to the island behind her so its quick dry material could do its job.

After rooting around in the kitchen, she found a serviceable pan, a disastrously dull knife, and everything she needed to actually serve. The olive oil in the cabinet was a horrible, tasteless light version, and she regretted not buying more essentials at the store. It would have to do. She put a couple eggs on to boil and let the salmon sit with salt, pepper, and fennel in a wash of that oil while she turned on heat under the pan, cubed up some of the bread, and toasted it with salt and pepper for croutons. She rinsed and dried the lettuce and cut up the rest of the produce, filling two shallow bowls to the brim.

She'd forgotten how much she liked cooking. The resulting food was good, of course, but it was also a dance around the kitchen, an efficiency of motion and timing, something between a sport and a game. The process of it was as soothing to her mind as a run along the lake. It had order and structure, this task, then this one, then that one, all with tangible results that served a purpose—and a higher one, Charlie thought when she heard the shower turn off. Feeding someone else was always a specific kind of pleasure, made her feel capable and necessary. And feeding Elizabeth… Charlie imagined Elizabeth standing just outside her shower, drying herself with a soft towel, her hair, made even darker by being wet, dripping on her shoulders, her breasts loose…

She pulled herself back to task, left the crouton crumbs in the pan, turned the heat down lower, and slid the salmon onto a hot sheen of oil skin side down. While it cooked, she sliced thick rounds of bread and popped them in the toaster. She hoped Elizabeth wouldn't take time to make herself up. Charlie had thought she'd looked incredible when they'd run into each other at 3 Greens, but now she wanted her naked face, wanted to have her relaxed from the run and shower. The best part of having a girlfriend was waking up next to her in the morning, mussed hair and pillow creases, slow smiles and un-messed-with beauty.

"That smells amazing."

Elizabeth's voice seemed to come from everywhere at once, but Charlie glanced up and noticed that the kitchen wall was lofted, leaving a gap between the top of the cabinets and the timber ceiling at least as tall as Charlie was. "Thanks. Five minutes. Do you usually eat at the island or the dining room table?"

"Um. The couch? Or my desk?"

"Am I going to have to teach you everything about food?" She pulled the egg pot off the stove and put it in the sink, running cool water into it.

"It's amazing I still eat real food at all. Did you know there are shakes out there that provide everything a body needs for the day? A couple guys at work swear by them."

"Eating is about more than sustenance."

"If all my meals smelled like that, I might agree." This time Elizabeth's voice came from Charlie's right, and she'd just lifted the pan of salmon from the heat when Elizabeth entered the kitchen and leaned against the island a few feet away. She was wearing a loose V-neck T-shirt and drawstring pants, and it was painfully obvious she had nothing on underneath. Charlie turned off the faucet.

"Have a seat." The toast popped up. "Do you want a job?" Before she could answer, Charlie fished the bread from the toaster, dropped it on a plate, and slid it over to Elizabeth along with a knife and a tub of something that was the closest thing to butter she could find. "Spread some of that on these."

"Yes, ma'am." Their gazes met, and Charlie felt her stomach drop and mouth go dry. She forced herself to swallow and remember the salmon and salads and time and space. When she turned from Elizabeth back to the counter, she took a deep breath, which reminded her that Elizabeth wasn't the only one who needed a shower after that run, no matter how much damage control she'd done at the kitchen sink. She reached over to grab her mostly dry top from the stool she'd hung it on and pulled it over her head. "Have you ever cooked on this stove? It's pristine."

"I've been known to scramble up some eggs."

"Are you sure that was in this apartment? It's beautiful, by the way. The wood and brick?"

"Thanks. I moved in a few years ago. It just…felt like home to me. I only wish I could spend more time here." The scrape of her knife across toasted bread stopped and was replaced by the crunching sound of a bite. Charlie glanced at Elizabeth over her shoulder; she had one hand covering her mouth, and the other held a piece of bread with a perfect half-moon missing from its side. "I'm starving," she said, the words muffled.

"Dinner's coming right up." Charlie peeled the eggs under cold running water, sliced them up, spread them across the tops of the salad bowls, and slid a fillet of salmon on top of each. She placed one bowl by Elizabeth and the other in front of the empty stool to her left. Two glasses of ice water and some knives and forks later, she settled into her spot, raised her glass, and said, "Bon appétit."

"This is incredible."

They both dug in. Elizabeth's enjoyment of the food was contagious, and they ate in a quiet that felt companionable until Charlie caught a glimpse of Elizabeth's cleavage down the neck of her T-shirt and registered the small sounds of satisfaction she voiced while chewing. The pleasure of it made it hard to swallow. When was the last time she'd felt any kind of desire, let alone something as intense as this?

At that thought, the quiet between them went from easy to thick. Each bite dripped with suspense, each sound she made was amplified until Elizabeth set her fork in her empty bowl and sighed. Charlie waited a beat, leaned over, and kissed her. They picked up where they'd left off by the front door. Elizabeth was a bouquet of creamy fennel and a coconut lotion laced with some kind of citrus. Charlie slid off her stool to get closer and pulled Elizabeth's hips toward her. They felt so good under her hands, had a give her own lacked. Elizabeth hooked one leg around Charlie's, and fingers played with the shaved hair at the back of her head.

"More," Elizabeth said. "I need more of you. Come with me."

They stumbled past the dining table to a couch in the living room that had gone dim with dusk. Elizabeth pushed Charlie down and lay on top of her. Their legs intertwined, and Elizabeth's thigh was hot against Charlie. Her back was smooth under Charlie's hands, her skin silky soft.

Elizabeth tugged at Charlie's shirt. "Take this off," she said, barely pulling her mouth from Charlie's to form the words. Charlie wanted to comply, but Elizabeth was all over her, lips moving from Charlie's mouth to her ear and then down to her neck. "Mm. Salty."

"I'm…"

"Come on." Elizabeth pulled at the hem of Charlie's shirt and sat up enough that Charlie could raise herself from the couch and yank it off over her head. The move was more than a little desperate and not sexy at all, and the cool air of the apartment against her skin woke her from her desire.

Elizabeth said, "I thought about you every night in California. You're so sexy."

"I'm smelly."

"Not really. I like it." She pulled her own shirt over her head. Oh, God. Charlie's hands were drawn to Elizabeth's breasts, and she was helpless to do anything but play her fingers down the curve of them, somehow expecting the freckles that dotted their creamy skin to have a different texture, tell her something in braille. Small nipples were a pinkish brown and crinkled under her touch and gaze. Elizabeth's breasts were soft but still firm, and they weighed in Charlie's hands perfectly. She wanted to take each of those pert nipples in her mouth and feel their hardness with her tongue, feel the change in breathing that her ministrations would evoke.

But when she started to sit up to take what she wanted, Elizabeth pressed her back down. "Let me touch you," she said.

"Oh, but…"

"I want to feel you." She tugged at Charlie's sports bra, which stayed welded to her chest. They struggled with it for a minute, their gyrations beating the tension and desire between them back from high flames into embers. It wasn't gone, not yet, but Charlie's bra was still covering one small breast when she said, "Wait. Just…"

"Why won't this thing come off?"

"Because it's still damp, and I'm lying down, and…"

Elizabeth made a growl that was so cute it made Charlie laugh.

"Don't! This is serious."

But then they were both laughing, tangled together on the couch. Their giggles felt as good as their kisses and rescued Charlie's want from the edge of oblivion. She kissed Elizabeth again, while tugging her bra back into place. Their kisses were long and deep. Unhurried. An end in and of themselves. "Yeah, like that," Charlie whispered and went back for more. Elizabeth's hands drifted to the waistband of her shorts, and Charlie reached down to stop them. "Can we just...Let's just do this for a while."

Elizabeth's answer was a crooked eyebrow.

"You feel so good, just like this. I want to savor it."

Elizabeth's expression said that she wanted to devour Charlie whole, which was exciting, but now Charlie was strangely committed to the idea of slowness, of not sprinting through discovering each other. They kissed until they were both flushed, hands roaming over skin and clothes, their thighs intertwined, the heat between them unbearable. Elizabeth made another play at Charlie's recalcitrant bra, and Charlie took the opportunity to lift one of Elizabeth's breasts to her mouth and dissolve into the pleasure of licking and sucking one hard nipple, then the other. It was as if that tasty dinner had only whetted her appetite, and this increased her hunger.

Elizabeth took in a deep breath and let it out in a low groan Charlie felt between her legs. She pulled back, which was one of the hardest things she'd done in her life. "Wow."

"Please tell me you're rethinking your take-it-slow idea."

Instead of answering, she sat up more, and Elizabeth slid off her. "I should go." Leaving was the only way she would not have sex with Elizabeth, and as much as she wanted just that, she liked the idea of an unfolding discovery, of playing out this teasing desire until it broke both of them. She found her shirt tucked under her and pulled it on. "You need some rest."

"As if I can sleep after this."

"I'm expecting some vivid dreams myself." She wanted to kiss Elizabeth again but made herself get up. "I'd stay and clean up the kitchen for you, but I'm afraid what'll happen."

"Whatever it is, it would be terrible." Sarcasm dripped from those words, half of which were muffled when she ducked her head into her shirt and yanked it down.

Charlie waited for her at the door. "I made enough for two more salads. Eat one tomorrow."

"I'm pretty sure you're only allowed to boss me around about running."

"You can't run if you don't eat. And sleep."

"And yet somehow I've done just that for the last month." Charlie knew Elizabeth's grumbles were at least partly an act, but based on the state of the refrigerator and the circles under Elizabeth's eyes, there was a hard kernel of truth under them, which was sobering.

"I'm serious. Take care of yourself."

"I do. I will."

Elizabeth's hand was on her doorknob when Charlie said, "When am I going to see you again?"

"I have to work tomorrow."

"On Sunday?" Elizabeth frowned and was about to say something, but Charlie stopped her. "Sorry. I promise not to be one of those people who gives you a hard time."

"Except about eating and sleeping."

"I *am* your running coach."

Instead of opening the door, Elizabeth kissed her again, backing Charlie up against the wood. How was such a petite woman so powerful? Charlie hadn't expected her to be so... aggressive, which was a stupid preconception, given her femininity. Charlie went along with Elizabeth's lips and tongue until her insides were molten. One of Elizabeth's hands had found the back of her head again and was drawing mesmerizing circles in the shorn hair there, making a soft rhythmic counterpoint to their mouths and breath. Somehow, Charlie found the will to put her hands on Elizabeth's shoulders and press as gently as she could. "Liz," she said. "Please."

"Still with the take-it-slow?"

"At least for tonight."

Elizabeth took a steadying breath and closed her eyes. "Your hair is so soft. And your lips." She said these things as if they were a surprise. Finally, she stepped back and opened the door. "I'll call you when I know about my schedule. Thank you for dinner. It was delicious. And so are you."

Charlie stepped out in the hall and watched Elizabeth close the door. The lock turned with a soft snick. Charlie let out a long breath. "Jesus."

"I heard that," Elizabeth said from the other side of the door.

"I'm leaving," Charlie said and quick-stepped to the elevator while she still could.

CHAPTER EIGHT

Nine Miles

Every Monday morning, Elizabeth sat across from Justin to review the train wreck of her schedule. This week was a morass of meetings, both in the office and around the city at current and potential clients, which left her little time for anything else, but someone had to follow up on the introductions she'd made at the conference. She sifted through her new followers and contacts on social media and worked with Justin to categorize them in two lists, ones Tyler could just get in their regular sales pipeline and others she wanted to take care of personally.

Justin rotated his laptop around so she could see the screen and pointed at the still-significant string of names and handles she'd kept aside for herself. "No one else can deal with those?"

"I'm pretty sure you're my assistant, not my mother."

He suddenly seemed nervous and adjusted the cornflower-blue tie he wore tied in a thick Windsor knot. Despite half her staff coming to the office in jeans and T-shirts (and some of them staying home and working in pajamas), Justin always wore slacks and a tie. It was his thing, and Elizabeth wondered how long he would hold on to it despite the prevailing winds of the tech hoodie culture. She hoped he would because the knot looked nice in his starched, spread collar, and she wondered if Charlie ever wore clothes like this. Cross-dressing to this degree would go well beyond butch, but if anyone could pull it off, Charlie could. She would be downright handsome. Dashing with her cheeky half smile.

Justin pulled her out of her brief reverie by saying, "I'm afraid I'm going to be forced to give my notice."

His words were a deluge of cold water on her thoughts. "What?"

"I promised myself I would leave if you didn't show any sign of changing."

"It's not your job to police me. If I want to work too hard, that's my business. I don't ask you to put in extra hours with me."

"No, but when you're gone, I have to deal with a constant stream of people wondering when you're going to get them whatever it is they want from you that you promised to them a week ago. Or a month ago. I can't do it anymore. It's like they think I have control over what you do and when you do it, and clearly I don't."

"Who's doing that? I'll get them to stop."

"What, are you going to fire the whole company so you can do *everything* yourself?"

They glared at each other across Elizabeth's desk. "Well, happy Monday to you too."

"I'm serious."

Elizabeth glanced away. "I know you are. Does it make any difference that I'm trying?"

"Not hard enough. We've all seen what you can do when you put your mind to it, so if nothing's happening, you're not really trying, are you?"

"I can't lose you. Not now. Tell me what I need to do to stop you from leaving."

Justin shifted in his seat and looked pained. "I don't want to make things worse for you. I don't. I like working here.

Everyone does. At least when you're letting them do their jobs. I thought things might change after you went to the hospital. I told myself and everyone else that I was sure things were going to change—"

"You told people I went to the hospital with a panic attack?"

He frowned. "Of course not. I just said that you and I had talked, and I'd been assured things were going to change. But now it's two months later, and literally nothing is different."

"I gave Dennis one of my conferences to go to." Only because she couldn't be two places at one time, she admitted to herself.

"I'm not here to argue with you."

Elizabeth leaned back and gazed up at the featureless ceiling. "I'm not arguing. Not really. Ah, Justin. Can you...Will you give me another month?"

"Will you hand off all the billable tasks on your plate right now?"

Elizabeth launched upright in her chair. "All of them? Hill and Berkowitz has been my client since the beginning."

"You can't tell me they need someone at your level doing that work."

"And yet they're more than happy to pay for it because they trust me."

"Hill of Beans will happily trust a senior consultant if you tell them to. And I said I'm not here to argue."

One of the major reasons Justin had lasted as her assistant for so long was his backbone, and she knew he wasn't kidding. She could feel her chest squeeze and throat tighten. A throbbing set up in her temples, and she gritted her teeth. "Okay, I'll do it."

"I'm not trying to change you, Elizabeth. I'm trying to quit."

"And I'm trying to stop you. If that means doing what I should've done a long time ago, so be it."

But he got up and placed a printed piece of paper on her desk. "My letter of resignation."

"Oh."

"I hope you make the changes you need to, but I got another offer last week, and I've decided to take it. I'll be here for two weeks to help you transition." He walked to her door. "I'm sorry. Do you want this opened or closed?"

"Closed, please."

He shut the door quietly, and Elizabeth sagged in defeat. What was she going to do? Carmen would tell her to do two things in quick succession: first, exactly what Justin had been waiting for her to do for the last two months, and second, get on her knees and start groveling to keep him. Offer him more money, more vacation, ownership in the company. But if he really wanted to leave, she wouldn't do that. Panic and overreaction were never practical responses. She could find another assistant, but that wasn't the point, was it? He was right, and Carmen was right, but she couldn't live her life on their terms, slow down in the exact way they said she should. She needed to find her own path to this different place they all wanted her in, but she needed to find it now.

Not surprisingly, she thought of Charlie again. Since Saturday night, Elizabeth had failed miserably at *not* thinking of her. It wasn't just her mouth or hands or legs that occupied her thoughts (and fantasies) but the way she'd taken care of Elizabeth, how she'd set up shop in Elizabeth's neglected kitchen and the nourishing food she'd made. There was something quietly *deliberate* about her that Elizabeth felt herself drawn to. Something sweetly thoughtful.

Charlie had said that difficulty was compelling, and that had struck a chord with Elizabeth, but she'd also talked about balance. Was it possible to have both? Could she push herself and the firm to walk this uncomfortable but thrilling bleeding edge, but let go at the same time? Step back? Take an entire weekend off? What did Charlie do with that seemingly endless stretch between five on Friday afternoon and nine Monday morning? How did she keep herself from getting bored? From examining mistakes and missteps and missed opportunities? Was her mind just that much quieter than Elizabeth's, or had she achieved the moving meditation she'd talked about across her whole life and not just on her runs? Elizabeth knew nothing about Charlie, really, and she wondered just how incompatible she'd find out they were over time.

The thought caused a resurgence of her tight-chested panic. She was flooded with memories of Carmen's many lectures of love, of her indelicate way of pointing out what she thought was Elizabeth's essential nature. Thought junkie. Perfectionist. Workaholic. Ms. X was out there, Carmen would assert, but you're not going to trip over her on your way from your office to the bathroom. Carmen wanted to hear the details of her kiss with Charlie, but would she think Charlie qualified as the missing variable from Elizabeth's life?

To beat back her sudden panic and doubt, Elizabeth thought about Charlie's voice, the way it had distracted her during that disastrous run, how Charlie had instructed her to manage her effort and the experience of her body. How she'd participated so wholeheartedly in their breathless kissing but had also embraced the idea of letting things last, of enjoying all of the different steps in the process.

Take it slow, she'd said. It was variation on what Carmen had been telling her for years, but hearing it in Charlie's voice, deep and soft with desire, made her actually want to comply. Breathe, she told herself. Ride out this panic. It'll pass. Justin will leave, but the world won't end. Change was possible, and Elizabeth would figure out how to do it in her way.

* * *

Veronica called Charlie into her office at the end of the day on Monday. "Close the door and sit down."

"Sure, but I think we're the only two people still here."

"Charlie, please." The tone of her voice was ominous, and Charlie knew what was coming before she closed the door and Veronica said, "We've decided to change and expand the role I was playing and are hiring someone from outside to fill it. The more Jennifer and I talked about it, the less it resembled what we'd been originally thinking, and it requires different skills than what you bring to the table."

Despite her initial reluctance about stepping up into a more demanding position, Charlie's disappointment was acute, but she tried to keep it from her face and voice. "Okay."

"But you know we're still growing and starting to get a footprint and real following in the northeast, so more opportunities are going to open up in the future."

"Hey, I get it."

"I just…You seemed excited about it, finally, and you know how much Jennifer appreciates what you've done for us all these years."

"Now it sounds like you're going to fire me."

Veronica laughed. "Oh, God. Never. You're a rock despite your irrational hatred of running skirts."

"Don't get me started." Charlie forced a smile she in no way felt and wondered how she'd ended up in the position of making Veronica feel better about this decision.

Veronica's laugh was a little too loud, and Charlie wondered when she could leave and feel quietly miserable by herself. "Well, listen. We're going to need your help getting this new person up to speed, and you know the ropes better than anyone. She doesn't start for a couple weeks and is much more into tennis than running—I may have finally found someone to challenge me on the court—but she wanted to join one of the group marathon sessions to get a feel for the community side of the business. I told her yours would be best and gave her your number to text for details. I think you're really going to like her."

Charlie wasn't sure how this could get any worse. Now they wanted her to be friends with the woman who'd stolen her job right out from under her? What was Veronica smoking? "Yeah, sure. Whatever you need."

Veronica tilted her head and squinted at Charlie. "Are you okay?"

The way she asked it meant she wasn't talking about the promotion she'd just ripped from Charlie's hands but was questioning Charlie's overall mental state. Charlie suddenly hated that Veronica knew about her condition, that she was, at times, her mother's spy into the otherwise safely opaque environment of RRiotWear. "I'm fine. Disappointed but fine. I'm sure this new woman's going to be great, and I'll make sure to get her whatever she needs to do a bang-up job." She was practically sweating with the effort to modulate her tone and inject some life and enthusiasm into it. She'd put on this act plenty of times over the years, but she wasn't sure if she was successful at it this time until she saw Veronica's face relax into a smile.

"Well, great. I knew you'd understand. You're the best, Chucky."

"Yeah, I know," she said, grinned sickly, and left the office and the building. She wanted to leave the whole city of Chicago, launch into space and go away, away, away. Either that or hunker down with Elizabeth on her couch with city lights sifting through her windows. Not kiss, not touch—or at least not in a sexual way—just...lie there. Being quiet. Was Elizabeth ever quiet? Did she ever turn off her scarily prodigious brain? Would she be interested in giving what Charlie craved right now?

They hadn't talked since Charlie had left her apartment, and even two days later, Charlie picked up her phone way too often, looking for texts or missed calls. How long did it take to check her schedule? Had the avalanche of work she'd gone back to buried her beyond the reach of this simple technology? Charlie hated feeling at Elizabeth's mercy but then wondered why she did. Elizabeth wasn't the only one with a phone. Charlie could text. She'd had the woman's nipple in her mouth, for God's sake.

She pulled her phone from her pocket and almost dropped it when it buzzed in her hands. Her heart jumped when she thought she'd conjured communication from Elizabeth out of thin air, but the text was from a number she didn't recognize.

Veronica told me I could contact you. This is Amber, the new sales and marketing director. I'm really excited to be joining the team... and to accompany you and your group on one of your runs. Jennifer and Veronica speak so highly of you. Maybe this Saturday? Please text with details.

Instead, Charlie wrote to Elizabeth and stood in the sunshine next to her building, waiting for an answer. *Shitty Monday. Don't suppose you're up for dinner out? Something easy.* If she got a yes, she'd walk south, across the river and into the Loop and to Elizabeth's building, which she'd found on the Internet. If she got a no, she'd walk east and then north, to the Red Line and her apartment, which she'd cleaned up in a bit of a frenzy on Sunday, imagining Elizabeth coming over and wanting to scrub the place of any evidence of her previous depression. It had taken most of the day, which had made it easier not to hear from Elizabeth, and the place looked as good as it ever did (though still hovel-like compared to Elizabeth's apartment), but she didn't want to go back there now.

Her phone was stubbornly silent, and she felt like an ass waiting around for a crumb from Elizabeth. They really weren't anything yet, she reminded herself. They might not ever be anything. Their desire might flame out when Elizabeth realized how far out of Charlie's mental league she was and Charlie got tired of being an afterthought to Elizabeth's admirable career. The woman ran her own business, and Charlie couldn't even get promoted. She slipped her phone in her pocket and headed to the Red Line.

She was almost at the station when it buzzed against her butt, and she pulled it out without slowing down. Elizabeth. *Shitty Monday squared. My assistant quit, and I'm scrambling. Dinner is what I want, but I need to stay here. This week is now officially a disaster, but I'm all yours after our run on Saturday. Tell me what happened to you.*

Charlie eased over to the edge of the sidewalk out of the heavy flow of foot traffic and read the text a few times. It was both perfect and infuriating. She wanted to play a little hard to get and delay her response, but she wrote: *Nothing as bad as that. Hang in there. Remember to eat. Saturday's a date.* But on Saturday, she had to deal with this Amber woman, job stealer, overenthusiastic suck-up. And her new boss? She hadn't even gotten that information from Veronica.

There wasn't enough Lithium in the world to lift her shitty mood, but Charlie reminded herself that wasn't the point. Feeling nothing was as bad as the heavy blanket of depression. Wasn't that the lesson her dad's suicide had taught her? He dreaded the void of his equilibrium, and though Charlie's dose was low and her medication gentle enough that it didn't make her feel numb (or at least just numb enough for it to be a relief), she wished for some anesthesia right now. In college, she would have drunk herself into a stupor; over the winter, she would have stirred up some boxed mac and cheese—if she could muster up the energy—and lose herself in *Law & Order* until she fell asleep. Today, she felt adrift.

Breathe, she told herself. She walked past the train station, crossed Michigan Ave., and cut over to the lake, like she'd led her running group those first two times. When she was on the path by the water, the breeze was brisk, and all around her were runners and cyclists, dog walkers and the occasional Rollerblader. Everyone was suddenly free from their workdays and outside, like they were all summer and fall in the city, soaking up sun and air and heat for the long, dark winter ahead. The wind had whipped up the lake, and waves crashed into the corrugated metal side of the built-up path, the largest ones spattering water up and over, darkening the concrete surface she walked on.

After a while, she called her mom. "I didn't get the promotion. They changed the job, and I was suddenly not qualified."

"Oh, honey."

"And now I'm going to have to show the ropes to the person who *did* get it."

"They shouldn't have asked you to do that."

"Who else was going to do it? It's still a small company. It makes a sick kind of sense, but I'm..." She squinted up at the pale sky, across which a few high clouds scuttled as if they were commuting home with everyone else.

"Are you okay?" The broken-record quality of this question (especially when she asked it of herself) was suddenly infuriating.

"I'm fine." The words came out loud enough to make a nearby runner turn his head. "Just mad, which is totally normal. I didn't tell you, but I just started a summer class at Northeastern. It's just a women's studies course that won't even get me closer to my degree, but I've been drifting for too long. I need to keep busy. Get motivated. Step things up a notch." Honestly, it'd been one of the easiest classes she could find, one with more reading than papers, and reading was one thing she could do no matter what.

"Okay..."

"I'm fine." She considered telling her mom about Elizabeth, but if work upheaval made her mom nervous, new relationships were even worse. Besides, she wasn't quite sure what was going on with her and Elizabeth anyway, so would be unable to either dismiss her mom's concerns or reassure her into resigned acceptance. "I'm thirty, though. I should want more than I have. I *do* want more. And I'm capable of having it without it sending me into the deep end. After all these years of therapy, I know myself."

Her mom backed off, and they talked about normal, easy things while Charlie covered a couple miles into Lincoln Park and the turnaround point to the last group run she'd done with Elizabeth. Maybe it was good she wasn't going to see her until Saturday. She could figure out how to finish her degree and get enrolled somewhere by then. She would have time to plan the perfect menu for after their run—delicious and nutritious, both. She'd pay her bills and hit the gym for a strength session or two. She'd do the small amount of homework that came along with this new class of hers. She'd keep busy.

* * *

Rain pinged off Elizabeth's car when she pulled into the lot by the totem pole for this week's nine-mile run. It was a warm rain, but it was still wet. That plus the uncharted distance and the wretched week she'd just had made her want to stay in her car, turn around, and spend the day in her apartment, which she'd barely seen the last two weeks. But, being with Charlie was enough of a draw to get her up and out, wincing when the first raindrops hit her head and shoulders. She tightened her ponytail and marched to their meeting spot, which was desolate in this weather.

Charlie was there, her running cap low over her face, her gray top—an old race T-shirt, from the printing on it—clinging to her shoulders, her shorts stuck to her thighs in a couple places. From this far away, she could easily be mistaken for a man, and Elizabeth was again confounded by her attraction, which flared up at the sight of Charlie's broad shoulders and strong legs. She was about to call out her name and get her attention but saw that she was talking to a woman Elizabeth hadn't seen before. She was feminine and athletic, decked out in RRiotWear's signature colors and a cute running skirt, and she leaned toward Charlie, laughing and smiling.

"Hey," Elizabeth said when she was close enough for it not to be a shout.

"Elizabeth." Charlie's grin was quick and genuine and made Elizabeth feel warm under the rain. "I'm glad you made it. Amber and I were just taking bets about how many people were going to bail because of the weather. Amber, this is Elizabeth, the most determined member of our group. Elizabeth, this is Amber. She'll be joining RRiotWear in a week as a director and my new boss."

They shook hands, and Elizabeth couldn't help but notice Amber's manicured nails. "Good to meet you," Amber said.

"Likewise."

"Determined, huh?"

"I tend to finish what I start."

Charlie hadn't made a move toward her at all, and Elizabeth figured she didn't want Amber to know about them. Were their dates somehow against company policy? That would seem like a ridiculous restriction, given that this was a running group and not an actual business. No money was exchanging hands, no contracts had been signed, and Charlie had no real power over them. Well, not officially, Elizabeth conceded when she found herself staring at Charlie's wrists, noticing how they were somehow both powerful and delicate.

"That's a good quality," Amber said, and Elizabeth felt a flare of annoyance.

"Elizabeth's not satisfied with just running a tech consulting firm, she has to add running a marathon to her impressive résumé too," Charlie said. Though Elizabeth generally didn't need—or want—anyone to stand up for her, she could have kissed Charlie right then.

"Wow, that's great."

They were saved from further small talk when two other members of the group showed up and got introduced. While the newcomers were talking with Amber, Charlie edged closer to Elizabeth and whispered, "She crashed the party, and I need to make a good impression."

"Are we still on for later?"

Charlie's smile was answer enough.

They started running in a few minutes, when half the group still hadn't shown up. Amber monopolized Charlie nearly the entire time, and Elizabeth started to wonder if Charlie was attracted to her. It was a silly thought, especially given that Amber was going to be Charlie's boss, but Elizabeth had a hard time controlling her mind after a few miles, when all the blood was shunted to her legs. The run was a wet slog, the rain cycling between light showers and brief downpours that left her feet sloshing in her soaked running shoes. She'd missed two workouts during the week, but this was going better than the Saturday run Charlie'd had to coach her through. Good thing, too, because Charlie was otherwise occupied this morning. Over the long nine miles, she only pulled herself away from Amber twice to talk with each of them during the walking breaks Elizabeth no longer needed or even wanted.

They ended up back at the totem pole, worse for wear, given the distance and the weather, and no one wanted to stay outside in the drizzle long enough to stretch. "I'll let you go only if you promise, *swear*, that you'll stretch right when you get home. I'm serious. I'll know if you don't. I'm like Santa."

They all chuckled and promised, making little crosses over their soaked chests. Elizabeth was about to give Charlie a pointed look about finally starting their date (she had a towel, a change of clothes, and makeup in her car), but Amber touched Charlie's arm and said, "Can I pick your brain over breakfast? Maybe we can both get dried off and meet somewhere convenient?"

"Uh, sure. Yeah. That's fine." She gave the briefest glance over to Elizabeth, paired with a spasm of her mouth that was probably meant to serve as an apology.

What in the world? Why was Charlie letting this woman walk all over her? She wasn't even officially her boss yet. They had plans. Plans that had been Elizabeth's lifeline through the whole shitty week. But then Elizabeth wondered how many times she'd canceled on Carmen or Jess or another girlfriend when something came up at her job, and she turned and walked to her car without another word or glance back.

She had work to do anyway, though the nature of it had changed slightly since Justin had given his notice. It had an end in sight, a finite target, a final goal: actually slowing down. Letting go. Fully training and trusting others. Now that she was as committed to that as this stupid marathon, she knew at least part of why she'd avoided doing it for so long. Some of it was her own type-A, control-freak nature, but the other part was that it was *hard*. How could she distill her experience and intuition into a method? A framework of thought that could serve to elevate and align her staff's existing strengths and intelligence. Because they were all smart and seasoned. They wouldn't be able to compete with the larger firms otherwise.

Given that her breakfast with Charlie had been usurped, Elizabeth actually stopped at the grocery store on the way home and proved the old adage true: never go shopping when you're hungry. She ended up at the checkout lane with a full cart and growling stomach. Her kitchen was going to be well stocked for the week; now all she had to do was actually eat what she'd bought instead of letting it go bad like all the other times she'd gotten a notion to stop throwing her money (and health) away on takeout.

At home, she ate a plate of eggs, seeded toast, and a bowl of fruit and yogurt while standing at the counter, reading through her email on her laptop. Charlie would want her to sit at a table, but one step at a time. In the quiet of her apartment, her plans ruined, Elizabeth finally understood how it felt to be on the receiving end of what she'd been dishing out her whole life, but this was only the smallest example of how she'd operated. Everything was on her terms and at her convenience, though it had never felt that way; it had always seemed necessary and uncontrollable. She'd imbued her work with a sense of importance nothing else could touch and had justified it by saying she was a public figure, a role model, an example that had to stay shining and inspiring. While an element of truth lurked in those ideas, she now felt how self-aggrandizing they really were.

To pull herself out of this funk of hard truth, she wanted to tell Charlie about this breakfast she'd made for herself, show her a picture of the food in her refrigerator, make "teacher" proud. But Charlie had her own life and career that was important to her—more important than an afternoon with Elizabeth—so she swallowed her disappointment, closed her laptop, and loaded her dishes in the dishwasher.

* * *

Charlie hadn't been able to rid herself of Amber until the early afternoon. The woman was tenacious, which was probably good from a marketing perspective but sucked when someone was trying to drain her brain of all her RRiotWear tribal knowledge. First it had been about company history and lore, then on to the actual merchandise, and then ahead to Charlie's ideas about community outreach and expanding into other regional markets. All the while, Amber had been clearly oblivious to Charlie's discomfort. Not just discomfort, but anger laced with a tired sadness.

Clearly Jennifer and Veronica hadn't read Amber in on Charlie's own ambitions for the job and had just assumed Charlie would accept this bait and switch and play nice. Why wouldn't they? That was exactly what Charlie had done, but, boy, it had been a bitter pill to swallow and had made her stomach churn through her veggie benedict and revolt halfway through one of

Ann Sather's famous cinnamon buns. She spent the next two hours nauseated and with a plastic smile fastened tight to her face but couldn't find the spine to shrug Amber off with the promise to work with her when she *actually started* at RRiotWear and help her get up to speed. Of course, then Amber would take the credit, and Charlie would be screwed again.

By the time she'd gotten home and taken a scalding shower, she felt like a failure twice over and had to at least pretend to meditate for a half hour to find some sort of equilibrium before calling Elizabeth to apologize for ditching her and see if she was around. She wasn't feeling remotely sexy but kept flashing back to that desire she'd had to lie on Elizabeth's couch with her and just be, breathing through sunset, warm and tight together. It was probably a good thing her call was sent to voice mail so she could avoid sounding too needy, but her follow-up text had also gone unanswered.

She wiled away the rest of the afternoon reading on her couch, resisting the siren song of her pajamas but not the urge to check her phone every fifteen minutes for something from Elizabeth. This was the second time she'd found herself in this position, and though she felt like a silly girl, she couldn't stop herself, even setting the phone next to the sink in the bathroom when she had to pee so she wouldn't miss Elizabeth's call. She reread the text she'd sent, checking that the tone was as light as she'd tried to keep it, but every time she looked at it, it sounded more and more desperate in her mind.

She told herself that she had other friends, even a few from outside RRiotWear; she could call one of them and meet for pastries and tea somewhere. Or catch a movie. Or browse the shelves at Women and Children First. She could go downtown and hit up a museum, though that seemed like an enormous amount of effort on such a lousy day. At the same time, she knew she'd ride down past the Loop to Elizabeth's place if she was summoned. Oh, how she wished Elizabeth would summon her.

Would they pick up where Charlie had made them leave off last week? She could still feel Elizabeth's weight on her, the heavenly press of her breasts against Charlie's fingers and tongue. Their kissing had practically undone Charlie, slow and thoroughly sensual. She remembered threading her fingers through Elizabeth's damp hair, the huff of her breath when Charlie had tugged it softly. Charlie wanted to feel the rest of her curves, hear the sounds she'd make when Charlie touched her everywhere. The thought sent shivers of electricity to her crotch. They would be glad they'd waited, but there was no reason to wait any longer.

She blinked her living room back into focus and wondered if Elizabeth had somehow come to the conclusion that Charlie was interested in Amber. The woman was nice enough despite being blind to Charlie's distress and was attractive, but she was also married with a kid, straight in every possible way. Besides, how could Charlie be interested in someone who'd stolen her job?

She kept herself busy with laundry and finally changing her closet and drawers over from winter to summer clothes, lugging plastic tubs and up and down from the basement until her forehead was damp with sweat and her arms were quiet with fatigue. She sank onto her couch with a sigh and went to put her feet up on her coffee table, but in front of her was her phone next to a short stack of feminist books for her course at Northeastern.

It was an evening class, so she wasn't the oldest person there, but that didn't quite abate her nervousness. Would she be able to handle it in addition to her job, which suddenly felt precarious and stressful on its own? Part of what had precipitated her downfall at college was the pressure of being a competitive athlete, but surely another part was the academics themselves. Midterm and final weeks had always been hard to take. But it was just one class. Elizabeth would tell her she could do it. If Elizabeth would talk to her.

She picked the top book off the pile and started reading, but her phone buzzed with a text before she was more than a paragraph in. Elizabeth, finally. *Sorry. I left my phone in the car and somehow didn't notice.*

Haha. I'm impressed you could survive without it for so long.

I was wondering why it was quiet in here. So, Amber?
I couldn't ditch her as easily as you left your phone.
I think she likes you. This was followed by a wink.

Charlie threw caution to the wind and called Elizabeth. "If she likes me, it's only because I know where all the RRiotWear skeletons are and how to get accounting to approve marketing expenses."

"Were you involved in her interviews?"

She couldn't quite stifle her disdainful laugh. "No."

"Oh? I feel like there's a story there."

"There is, but I'm dealing with it."

"Charlie." Elizabeth's breath was a faint rush over the phone. "Tell me."

So, Charlie did, starting with "Remember when I said Monday was a shitty day?" and going forward from there. She told Elizabeth the whole story. Well, almost. She skipped the part about her lack of a college degree and the damning detail of having waited so long to pursue the promotion in the first place. Elizabeth made sympathetic noises throughout, and Charlie felt some of her indignation and disappointment unfurl into something more quiet and less destructive within her.

At the same time, Elizabeth got more and more worked up. "Now this Amber woman is taking advantage of you to make herself look good?"

Charlie sighed. "I don't think it's that. She's just excited."

"Are you saying that because she's a woman?"

"I…what?"

"If Amber was a man, would you think he was just excited or that he was plotting his way to the top?"

Elizabeth's question made Charlie glance over at the women's studies books she was working through and grimace. "Okay, point taken. It's just that RRiotWear isn't really that kind of place. You know, world domination and squash the competition." Which, of course, was one big reason Charlie had been there for so long.

"If you insist. Just know that I'm offended on your behalf. I may even boycott you guys for a while."

"Uh, they do still pay for my rent and food."

"Point taken. How do I make this better for you?"

"Honestly, you already have. But maybe come over for breakfast tomorrow? I have enough grub here to feed an army… or a hungry CEO."

Elizabeth's sigh was loud and long. "I have to work. Believe me, I'd rather not, but my back's up against it."

"It's okay," Charlie rushed to say even though it felt far from it.

"How about dinner later in the week? I should be able to have enough things under control by then."

"It's a date."

They hung up, and Charlie lay back against the couch. Her brain was a kaleidoscope of feelings too mixed up to address one at a time. Talking with Elizabeth had taken some of the sting out of the Amber situation, but she couldn't help but wonder why Elizabeth insisted on working over the weekend when she didn't seem to want to. Or was her sigh and resigned tone just a ploy to make Charlie think she *had* to put in those hours, but that really, Elizabeth preferred to work over being with her? Or maybe Charlie's nerves about work and this class had gotten to her, and she was thinking about this too much. She put her phone down, picked up her book, and resumed reading, trading a fruitless distraction for a productive one.

CHAPTER NINE

Ten Miles

Charlie's mom had decided to extend her Fourth of July visit, taking the train in after work on Wednesday and keeping Charlie's sofa bed occupied until Sunday. While Charlie was at work, her mom took in the many museums around the city before they met up for dinner in a different neighborhood every night: Ukrainian Village, Logan Square, Hyde Park, Pilsen. Charlie loved her mom, and she made good company all around—at least when she wasn't distracted with worry about Charlie's mental state—but Charlie had to forgo her date with Elizabeth because of the visit. It was starting to feel like the universe was conspiring against them.

She could've invited Elizabeth along on one of their dining adventures; Elizabeth would have knocked her mom's socks off, but it was too early for that. Besides, the last thing Charlie wanted to do was incite her mom's concern, and new relationships always put her on edge—for good reason. Charlie's track record was less than stellar, and though the fact was that most relationships ended (hell, even most *marriages* ended), Charlie's tended to end badly and, more often than not, involved a depressive episode or two as the trigger for the beginning of the end. Or the end of the end.

Her strategy to keep Elizabeth from her mom was short-lived, though, when Saturday morning brought with it the first double-digit run of the training season followed by RRiotWear's inaugural friends and family picnic. Charlie tried to downplay it, but her mom was having none of it. "Am I not your family? Don't you need another set of hands to help out?" So, when Charlie jogged off to meet her group at the totem pole, her mom walked to Montrose Beach, where the RRiotWear people who weren't leading training groups were setting up tables and merchandise and organizing caterers and entertainment.

Charlie was a couple minutes late, and everyone in her group was there, huddled together, looking nervous. She laughed. "And this is why people say that the marathon is ninety percent mental. Don't you guys remember running nine miles last week? At least those of you who braved the rain to be with me? This is just one more. You've all got this. I promise."

Elizabeth smiled but hung back, and Charlie wondered at her shyness. Did she not want the group to know they'd started dating? She wore a spaghetti-strapped tank top, and her shoulders glistened with the pale sheen of sunblock—something Charlie had forgotten to apply before dashing out the door. She'd surely be a little pink after these miles and the subsequent picnic. They took off south along the lake, and Charlie made herself talk to Jamie and Julie before falling in next to Elizabeth at the back of the pack.

"I missed you," she said.

"I was forced to make my own salmon salad." Elizabeth huffed a few breaths before continuing, "It wasn't nearly as good as yours."

"You cooked?" Charlie made her face into a look of shock and drifted closer to bump Elizabeth on the shoulder. Even that small, innocuous contact made her remember Elizabeth's weight on her two weeks before and the silky feel of her breasts. She shivered in the heat.

"See what you've done to me?"

"You're amazing. I can't even guess what you're going to do next."

"Probably backslide into old habits, so don't get too excited."

"I doubt that. So...my mom's going to be at the picnic."

Elizabeth glanced over at her.

"You'll like her."

Elizabeth laughed. "I don't think that's the issue."

"She'll like you. I tried to get her to go to a museum. She loves museums. But she wanted to help, so what could I say?" They ran a long minute in silence. "We don't have to tell her anything about us. You can just be my group member."

"We'll see."

It shouldn't have surprised her that Elizabeth wasn't enthusiastic about meeting Charlie's only family, but she spent the next couple miles worrying about it. They were a few water stops into the run when Charlie drifted next to Elizabeth again. Sweat was beaded on her shoulders and chest and running in streaks down her face, curling the dark hair at her temples that was loose from her ponytail.

Elizabeth said, "Carmen's going to be there too. She knows a little about us."

"How little?"

"Just that we kissed." Charlie glanced over and saw Elizabeth's smile exaggerate the pink curve of her cheek. "She was surprised but happy."

"Why surprised?"

"You're...not my usual type."

Charlie grinned. "You mean like Jessie?"

"Carmen thinks you're hot."

"I like her already. But what about you?"

Elizabeth blurted out a laugh. "I'm trying to run, here," she said.

The thing was that Elizabeth was exactly Charlie's type, and her mom knew it. If she caught one lingering look between them, she'd deduce what was going on, no matter how they played it. And as soon as they were out of earshot of Elizabeth, the interrogation would begin: how long had they been seeing each other, how serious was it, was Charlie just an experiment for her, did she *know*?

Charlie was sure of one thing. There was never the "right" time to tell someone you struggled with mental health issues. Try it too soon, and you'll scare them off, but if you wait too long, they'll feel like you've been lying to them. Besides, the longer she left it, the greater the probability that she'd slide into an episodic depression, which was anywhere between challenging and impossible to hide. Buying time to make this disclosure before things got too serious between them had been one reason Charlie had wanted to take things slow with Elizabeth. In fact, she'd meant to take things even a little more slowly than they had, though now their schedules (and her mother) made her wish she'd succumbed to desire on Elizabeth's couch two weeks before.

Charlie knew her mom would be tempted to find out how much Charlie had told Elizabeth, and she spent the second half of the run alternating between encouraging her charges to conquer this uncharted territory and strategizing how to keep her mom off the scent of her burgeoning relationship with Elizabeth—or, failing that, avoiding a situation where she spilled the beans about Charlie's circumstances, whether inadvertently or as a premeditated challenge.

* * *

Elizabeth had thought she'd gotten away with the most cursory meeting of Charlie's charming but somehow intimidating mom, given the energy and activity of the RRiotWear picnic, but just as she was edging closer to Charlie to say goodbye and try to firm up a date when they could get together, just the two of them, the woman appeared out of nowhere, smiling in a way Elizabeth suspected wasn't entirely genuine. She was tall with narrow shoulders and wide hips that were pleasantly maternal-looking, but her hair was steel gray and her gaze more direct than social. "Elizabeth, would you care to join Charlie and me for dessert? There's that Swedish bakery by her apartment I've been dying to try, and you all must be hungry after your run."

In fact, Elizabeth had done a bang-up job stuffing her face with the spread RRiotWear had provided—turkey sandwiches, oranges, jumbo bags of chips, and cookies—and wasn't hungry in the least, but as she was formulating the just-right way to decline the invitation, Carmen piped up. "Can I crash the party? I'm one of those people who run so I can eat, not the other way around."

"Of course," Charlie's mom said. "The more the merrier."

Charlie said, "Maybe we should invite Veronica."

"Oh, I think she's still busy here, and she mentioned she needed to get to her son's baseball game after this."

"Maybe these guys want to clean up a little. It was a long, hot run, and—"

Carmen interrupted. "Oh, no. We're fine. We're not those women who won't be seen in public without their full makeup on. Don't you have a change of clothes in your car, Elizabeth?"

She did, in fact, have a change of clothes as well as a travel bag of toiletries in her trunk with the thought of spending the rest of the afternoon with Charlie and picking up where they'd left off two weeks before. If that wasn't on the menu, she should probably get some work done, but it was clear she and Charlie were being railroaded into this outing, so she succumbed. "All I need is five minutes in a bathroom somewhere, and I'll be good as new."

"That makes one of us," Charlie said. "But at least I can stop at home on the way over. I need to help out here a little bit, but do you guys want to meet up in a half hour?"

After a little more coordination, Elizabeth found herself walking to Carmen's car, since it was closer than her own. "What were you thinking?"

"I was thinking you needed a buffer. That woman is intense."

"I was perfectly capable of getting myself out of the whole thing before you butted in."

"Right. Keep telling yourself that. Anyway, it'll be fine. You've been in stickier situations before, and I'll diffuse her attention."

They settled into Carmen's sedan, and she started the engine. The vents blasted hot air at them before Carmen turned the fan down. Into the sudden quiet, Elizabeth said, "I haven't met a girlfriend's mother in at least a decade."

"You'll do fine."

And, for the most part, she did. After Carmen drove Elizabeth to her car and they both made their way over to Andersonville, the four of them crowded around a small table with an array of pastries, and Carmen was brilliant at changing the focus of the conversation whenever Charlie's mom leaned toward Elizabeth with an expectant look on her face. They talked about running and the weather, which was supposed to turn hot and sticky in a couple days, and the evolution of workout gear into garments of style and, for better or worse, prevalence.

Charlie seemed like a different person around her mother, and Elizabeth was reminded of how Carmen always said she got "snotty" around her parents. Something indelible happened between parents and children during adolescence that informed all their future interactions. Instead of snotty or argumentative (like Carmen got with her own parents), Charlie became quiet and little deferential. She corrected her mom regularly but with some delicacy when the woman regaled them with stories of Charlie's athletic prowess in high school. Her glances at Elizabeth across the table were quick and almost furtive.

At a pause in the conversation, Charlie's mom asked Elizabeth and Carmen, "Now, where did you two meet? Because it seems like you've been friends a long time."

"Longer than we like to admit at this point," Carmen said with a laugh. "We met in college. Sophomore year at MIT. I walked into my dorm room and there she was, computer nerd and scholarship kid but still able to hold a normal conversation. You have no idea what a relief it was. To both of us! Two relatively normal girls at that school. Well, normal as you can be there. Both our roommates before had been horror shows, honestly. Talk about socially awkward."

While Carmen spoke, Elizabeth watched Charlie's shoulders pull into each other and her chin dip to her chest. She took a sudden and engrossing interest in her fingernails, and Elizabeth wished to God that Carmen would shut up. She didn't know why this revelation of their history was bothering Charlie, but it clearly was, and Elizabeth could see Charlie's mom shooting glances around the table with a smile that was too static to be real. The whole thing reminded her of Charlie's hurry to leave 3 Greens the night of that waste-of-time interview.

She interjected before things could get worse. "But that was a long time ago. Ancient history, though sometimes it does feel like just yesterday. Time does funny things when you keep too busy, right?" She checked her watch, which she'd picked up at Fleet Feet with these shoes that she now loved. "In fact, I should really get going. I need to hit the grocery store and have some work to do. Besides, we've already intruded too much on family time." She scooted her chair back and dug through her pockets. "Let me just find some cash for our part of the bill."

"Oh, no," Charlie's mom said. "I invited you girls out, so it's on me. Charlie, why don't you walk Elizabeth to her car while I settle things here."

That suggestion said everything; if they thought they'd kept their attraction from Charlie's mom over the last hour, they were dead wrong. She and Charlie got up at the same time and headed out of the bakery without a word. Once they were past the large front windows, Charlie said, "I'm sorry. She can—"

"No, no. It's okay. She was fine. I mean, kind of frightening, but fine."

"She's overprotective of me. It's because—"

"Really, it was okay. I wish Carmen hadn't gone on and on about our college days, but when she gets on a roll, it's hard to stop her. It wasn't quite how I imagined spending the afternoon with you, but you *are* kind of cute when you get embarrassed." She reached out and captured Charlie's hand. The feel of their fingers intertwining sent a shiver of electricity up Elizabeth's arm. "How long is she staying?" she asked in a low voice.

"Too long. Until late tomorrow. Are you free at all this week? Dinner one night?"

They'd arrived at Elizabeth's car on a quiet side street. "Yes. I'll have to check my schedule, but yes." They faced each other, close enough that the air between them grew dense and still. "I've been waiting hours to kiss you."

She wrapped her arms around Charlie's neck and pulled her down. Their kiss unlocked the desire that Elizabeth had kept tamped down around Charlie's mom and Carmen. Her hand gravitated to the back of Charlie's head and the short but velvety hair there. It was like Charlie distilled down to the microcosm of a couple inches of skin and forest of follicles. Incongruous but addictive. Everything about her was this yin-yang of an androgyny laced with an undeniable feminine energy. Charlie's arms strengthened around her, and breath escaped her in a moan. The way Charlie's tongue sought hers out held the same powerful ease as her running stride. She melted into their kiss, letting it spark desire all the way through her. But she finally remembered that they were on a public street and managed to pull away.

"My back seat's pretty roomy. It's actually one of the car's selling points."

Charlie pressed her forehead against Elizabeth's. "Believe me. It's tempting."

"This taking it slow is driving me crazy."

"Honestly, this might be a little slower than I'd anticipated." But Charlie smiled when she said it, and Elizabeth felt her desire morph into something different: warmer and more expansive.

"Ah, Charlie. You do something to me."

"Given the opportunity, I'd like to do a whole lot more." She laughed and stepped back. But that wasn't what Elizabeth had meant; she'd meant the flutter in her chest and the lightness in her limbs when she climbed into the car after another brief kiss.

She was still thinking about it when Carmen called her. "Okay, what's really going on with you and Charlie?"

"I told you before that we'd kissed."

"Lizzie, I saw the way you looked at her. You actually

blushed one time. And that thing you came out with about needing to go to the grocery store? That was either true or you said it to impress Charlie's mom. Either way, it means you're not yourself."

Elizabeth turned onto Lake Shore Drive and sped along next to the path she'd just run down. She told Carmen she was making something out of nothing, but she went on to recount her run with Charlie two weeks before, the amazing dinner Charlie had made, their hot make-out session on the couch, the embarrassing size of her desire to see Charlie the next week, her disappointment at Charlie choosing her not-yet boss over her, and her chagrin at understanding she was on the receiving end of what she'd pretty much constantly dished out to her girlfriends her entire life. Once she'd started talking, the words tumbled out of her until, finally, she'd said it all.

After a long pause, Carmen said, "Wow. Wow, wow, wow. You're really falling for her."

"I'm—"

"Don't argue with me. I knew your panties were on fire over her, and she's charming in her butchy way, but I didn't know you'd gotten all romantic too. At least your brain is admirably uninvolved."

"Why do you say that?"

"Because Charlie's nothing like Sharon Stackhouse, who wouldn't be caught dead coaching beginning runners to their first marathon."

Right. Elizabeth couldn't deny her own romantic history, her thought-junkie ways. She'd never understood how anyone could pair off with someone who didn't spark an intellectual stimulation that would outlast the hot flame of new desire. But with Charlie… "She's different. The way she made me dinner, how she talked on that run, her focus, the questions she asks…"

"Lizzie. You know I love you. I do." Here it goes, Elizabeth thought. "And I think you're wonderful. But *do not* fuck around with this woman."

"I'm not fucking around with her! We're not even fucking." At least not yet, unfortunately.

"You're about to, whether you admit it or not. You're going

to make her fall in love with you, and then you'll figure out she's not Sharon-caliber, and you'll break her heart."

Elizabeth changed lanes and sped up, trying to outrun Carmen's words. "I'm not hung up on Sharon."

"No, but you're hung up on the idea of her. Of the mythic quality your life would have if you were with someone like her. The ultimate intellectual seriousness of it."

"I don't think mythic—"

"You might know what you want, but you don't know what you need. You're crazy brilliant, but I've been waiting for you to figure yourself out for almost twenty years. You need balance, but you clearly don't want it. Which means you're going to get to some point with Charlie where you realize she doesn't fit into your strict definition of the life you *should* be living, and you'll dump her."

"I don't always dump people."

"No, sometimes you drive them to leave you."

Elizabeth straightened her arms and pushed herself back into her leather seat while trying to formulate a response that didn't sound as defensive as she felt. Everything in the apartment she was driving too quickly toward was *just so*. Tidy. Un-lived-in. At least her home office was thick with equipment and cords and, always, an open notepad to catch ideas about new frontiers or techniques, but what did that say about her? She tried to imagine herself and Charlie on the couch on a quiet Sunday morning…doing what? Would she be able to relax and not work? Just…be? It sounded both compelling and impossible.

She breathed in and out. "I've just had to work so hard to get to where I am."

"I'm not denying that. But you've made it. Maybe now you can stop pushing so hard."

The words *It's not that easy* stampeded across her brain, but she swallowed them. "Maybe." This day wasn't going at all the way she'd thought it would, or how she'd wanted it to, needed it to. "Listen, I have to go and pick up some things at the grocery, which wasn't a lie or a ploy or however you interpreted it." While she *was* planning on stopping at Whole Foods for provisions for the week, she was perfectly capable of talking while driving or wandering the store aisles, but Carmen took the hint and said goodbye, but not before apologizing the way she always did when she'd gotten on Elizabeth's case too hard and for too long. Elizabeth stewed on the way to the store, when forking over way too much money for way too little food, and while drowning her frustrations in a long shower, trying to focus on the driving beat of the hot water against her back instead of a percolating panic that Carmen was right.

She was trying to change, but the tightness in her chest echoed Carmen's sentiment. Was she really at a place in her career where she could step back? Or at least stop stepping forward so insistently? Even if she was, could she find a way to do it? Justin had faith in her ability to move mountains if she only wanted to, but this wasn't a technical problem or recalcitrant client. This wasn't business, it was… Her confidence didn't extend out to these rarely charted territories, and if she couldn't figure out a way to make the changes she was supposed to, and if she wasn't sure Carmen was wrong about her "Sharon fixation," was it fair to lead Charlie on? Her heart squeezed at the thought. There was no denying it: she was falling for the woman. Which meant that Carmen was right, no matter how little Elizabeth wanted to admit it. If she was ultimately going to lead Charlie on and break her heart, she had to do what every cell in her body wanted her not to. She had to protect Charlie from herself.

CHAPTER TEN

Half Marathon

Two weeks later, Charlie walked from RRiotWear across the river and into the Loop, directly to Elizabeth's building. She had spent too much time looking at The McIntyre Group's website, gazing at Elizabeth's face on the "Our Team" page and browsing through pictures of their space, even reading each product and service description. She hadn't heard from Elizabeth since saying goodbye after they'd sat with her mom at the bakery, let alone seen her at the totem pole for the last two group runs. She wasn't sure what had gone wrong, but how could she when Elizabeth refused to answer the phone or respond to a text? Charlie hadn't read the signals wrong, *couldn't* have, not with the way they'd gone at it on Elizabeth's couch, how they'd kissed outside Elizabeth's car, but something had happened without Charlie knowing about it, and over the last two weeks, she'd gone from worried to stinging with disappointment to angry at being ghosted.

When she'd made it back to the bakery that day, she'd given her mom a hard time about the multitude of things that should have gone differently during that little orchestrated sit-down, but there'd been no real venom behind it, not with that kiss so fresh in her memory, not with the feeling of Elizabeth's body imprinted on the insides of her arms.

She was sure she was smiling even when she said, "And all that stuff about my high-school glory days?"

Her mom closed her pocketbook and looked at Charlie. "I don't think that Elizabeth is good for you."

"That's because you don't think anyone is good for me."

"That's not true. There's nothing more I'd like to see than you being with someone who cares about you. Who's on the same wavelength. Who can handle—"

"I don't need to be handled." Charlie's joy slipped a notch at this old argument.

"That's not what I meant." Her mom got up and walked past Charlie out of the bakery. "But did you hear all that talk about MIT? She's clearly very invested in her work, and where does that leave you?"

Charlie followed her down the sidewalk. "She's making changes. Besides, it's barely anything right now. We've hardly even gotten started." Which was a lie given how her mom's words stung. Her mom glanced over, and Charlie knew she saw right through her. "I can take care of myself."

But the kernel of doubt that conversation had planted grew like a weed until it had obliterated the sun and had proven her mom correct again. Now, almost two weeks later, Charlie told herself to let it go, ignore the desire she knew Elizabeth had felt for her, forget the emotional resonance she swore had hummed between them, and focus on the trepidation that had washed over her at Elizabeth's academic history and the fear of disclosing her mental struggles. She told herself this, but her feet were insistent on taking her to Dearborn Street after work this Friday, where Elizabeth was surely slaving away on the twenty-first floor. She stood outside the building's glass entrance, watching people flow in and out of its revolving doors—generally out at this time of the day. Most of the guys were dressed like her: buttoned shirts rolled up at the sleeves to the beautiful July day, slacks settling in drapes over black and brown shoes, oxfords, wingtips, monk straps. Today hers were brown-and-white saddle shoes that were her mom's favorite.

A man wearing jeans and a T-shirt pushed his way through the revolving door with his eyes on his phone and a McIntyre Group messenger bag slung over his shoulder. Charlie shoved her hands in her pockets and was about to slink away and forget she'd ever acted on this terrible impulse when she saw Elizabeth exit the elevators and turn toward her. She wore a green summer dress and carried her own McIntyre Group bag by the handle like it was a briefcase. She said something to the security guard standing behind the building's reception area desk. Her hair was in a braid, and her eyes crinkled with her smile. Charlie turned away abruptly and hurried down the block so Elizabeth wouldn't see her.

But she wasn't even a full building away when Charlie heard her name. She thought about pretending she hadn't and ducking around the next corner and into a building in case Elizabeth was actually following her, but hadn't she been the one skulking around? She stopped and turned, and her throat thickened at the sight of Elizabeth, her quick stride and serious face. "Hey," she said when Elizabeth got closer.

"I've been meaning to call, but I—"

"Don't worry about it. I get it. You don't need to spell it out."

"Charlie."

"Liz." She tried to give it the sound of a sneer, but she probably failed.

"Will you let me explain?"

"You don't have to explain. I got the message."

Elizabeth's eyebrows pulled together, and her gaze dropped to her heels. "I know I behaved poorly, but I didn't want to drag you into my stuff, and I couldn't figure out how to explain—"

"That it's not me, it's you?" Charlie's arms had crossed in front of her chest of their own accord.

"In a way."

"Like I said, I got the message." She glanced down at her watch without even looking at the time it showed. "I have to go." She took one more wretched look at Elizabeth and turned away.

"I didn't stop running," Elizabeth called after her.

"Good for you," Charlie said without turning back. She ducked around the block and out of sight and jogged past a few buildings to get lost in the foot traffic on State Street. Though she was right by a Red Line stop, she walked north, back toward the river, steaming along the sidewalk, weaving through other pedestrians—commuters and shoppers, both. Why had she done that? What had she thought was going to happen, that Elizabeth would soften at the sight of her, would trot out the just-right reason for why she hadn't called? Stupid, she thought, which was exactly how she'd felt in that bakery when Carmen had talked about their time at MIT. Or, if not stupid, then at least a fearful liar. When kissing Elizabeth at her car after escaping from Charlie's mom, Charlie had promised herself she'd tell Elizabeth the truth about her situation the next time they were alone together, even if it drove her away. But somehow she'd been driven away even without knowing the unsavory bits of Charlie's history.

Her situation. Right now, her situation was less her lack of a college degree or her bipolar designation (that was beaten into submission by a seventy-year-old drug) than her being burned by Elizabeth. What had happened? There'd been something there, something beyond mere lust. Charlie would've sworn on it. Something both easy and exciting. Something that was, Elizabeth now insisted without really insisting, actually nothing.

Over the last couple weeks, the rest of Charlie's life had started to settle down, but Elizabeth's absence had grown into an unscratchable itch. Even as she got used to working for Amber instead of Veronica, her spasms of anger evening out into resignation, even as she remembered that she actually liked the job she was currently doing, even as she lost her nervousness about this one class she was taking and could focus on the material instead of the possibility of failure, the specter of Elizabeth demanded her attention.

Now, there was no denying reality, no miraculous excuse that would reconcile Elizabeth's silence with somehow continued affection. The summer sun beat down on Charlie when she crossed Wacker to the river, and her frenetic pace slowed, though not before it had raised sweat on her back and under her arms, dampening her shirt. She loosened another button below her collar to encourage some airflow against her chest and told herself to forget about Elizabeth. Charlie's life was good without her. She was getting back in shape, things had reclaimed a new normal at her job, she had a plan to finish her degree, which might open up other opportunities for her. Her mood was stable, and summer in Chicago was full of things to do: concerts, festivals, dining outside, savoring the long evening light.

She should call one of her friends to get together. Or study by the lake. Or find a new recipe and shop for unfamiliar ingredients. But she stood rooted on the bridge, watching the river flow below her, away from the lake, opposite to its intended direction. She pictured herself and Elizabeth approaching this bridge down below on the river walk during their run together, Charlie coaching her through the low point and the rest of her miles. Just like those miles and that challenging run, this would pass. Everything passed: her depression, her mania, miles under her feet, her father from this world.

Charlie would forget about Elizabeth eventually. But sometimes eventually felt like a very long time.

* * *

Elizabeth had left work by six every day that week, a feat she'd never accomplished before—except maybe around Christmas when everything was slow and her work so uninterrupted that the quiet of the office became practically unnerving early in the evening. She'd been proud of herself, almost gleeful, until she'd seen Charlie, frowning magnificently before running away from her. Well, not running, of course. If Charlie had wanted to, she could put some real distance between them. Elizabeth had seen how quickly she could move on one of the group runs, when she'd applied a burst of speed over the last quarter mile on a dare. Her legs had looked so lean and fast, her feet barely brushing the ground before kicking back up almost to her butt, and she had moved with a propulsive grace.

According to Carmen, Elizabeth shouldn't have tried to follow her, shouldn't have forced that horrible conversation where she could see how badly she'd fucked up. But the sight of Charlie had hit her hard, making her heart jump into her throat, sparking an excitement and happiness she only remembered a moment later weren't hers to feel. Charlie's quiet anger was justified and probably permanent, but Elizabeth wanted to pretend it wasn't. She needed to believe something was possible between them because it was that thought that helped power the changes she was trying to make, the changes she knew were necessary before being with Charlie, being with *anyone*, was possible.

She was in the process of hiring two more consultants to pick up different parts of the hands-on work she still spent too much time doing. It would take weeks, maybe even months to find the right people, but she was determined. She'd handed off more conference appearances and had transitioned the Hill of Beans account to a managing partner who had been underutilized. These weeks had been full of client hand-holding, company meetings, and interviews for consultants and Justin's replacement, but her evenings had been resoundingly quiet, the hours spinning out so slowly from six to when she could manage to fall asleep after midnight.

She had no idea how to be with herself when she wasn't working, how to spend that time *not* getting one more thing done or planning how to tackle the next. The hours threatened to drive her crazy, but she found videos on yoga and meditation, checked books out from the library, and did whatever she needed to in order not to work. It was as much of a detox as if she was physically addicted to alcohol or drugs, and for the past two weeks, she'd had serious doubts that she could make it through to some more quiet, balanced life.

In moments of total defeat, she lay on her couch and let herself think of Charlie. Her smile was always the gateway into

Elizabeth's fantasies. First the half one with the almost dimple, and then when she fully lit up, her dark eyes sparkling with it. It felt like victory to elicit that smile and her low laugh. But the smile led to her kisses, long and slow and deep, and then Elizabeth was gone into the deliciousness of imagination. She ached to finally feel Charlie's breasts, to taste that soft skin that was always hidden away. She'd run her fingers down Charlie's trim stomach, feeling the strong muscles beneath that were sheathed in velvet flesh that mirrored that delicate hair on the back of her head.

Elizabeth succumbed to fantasy, touching herself first as she imagined caressing Charlie and then as she ached to have Charlie attend to her. It would be so easy, wouldn't it? Charlie knew bodies, was a master at warming up and finding the right pace. Her mouth had been so knowing, her tongue bringing Elizabeth to a flush of desire. The way her lips had played over her breasts that night... Elizabeth groaned at the memory and felt herself grow wet. Charlie had taken her nipples with such naked need and pleasure. She imagined Charlie kissing her way down her body, across her hip, to the inside of her thighs, making murmurs and moans of appreciation just like she had that night.

Elizabeth's hand found her own wet heat while she imagined Charlie taking her in her mouth, her tongue exploring, her hands cupping her hips, her belly. Her body was on fire, and she pushed inside herself, imagining Charlie doing the same. She could hear Charlie's low hums of pleasure, feel the knowing warmth of her tongue. She stroked herself, her body tightening, her heart pounding, engulfed in memory and fantasy, until she cried out when she came, her body shuddering and the spell broken. She'd stopped them before they'd even gotten started, and she'd never be the one to make Charlie smile again, to make her breath catch when they kissed. She lay on the couch, bereft and lost.

But this morning, she'd woken up actually feeling rested, her four-mile run had been along a lake that was calm as glass, and she realized that the fog of overwork had lifted from her mind and that the key wasn't necessarily just *less* but also *different*, where different equated to a mental flexibility she'd maybe never had. While running south past Buckingham Fountain, the rush of traffic on Lake Shore Drive picking up in the morning commute, Elizabeth had caught herself imagining lying on the couch with Charlie. Maybe Charlie would be reading a book or magazine or listening to a podcast with headphones while Elizabeth chipped away at an article or new conference presentation, together in an easy way that didn't require either of them to give up who they were.

But then she'd look at Charlie or Charlie would look at her, and they would abandon their separate tasks to kiss and touch, shedding clothes like she'd wanted to do so badly that night. She imagined Charlie's hands in her hair, whispering something Elizabeth wanted to hear but maybe didn't need to, imagined her fingers inside Charlie, the easy abandon she knew Charlie would have to the pleasure Elizabeth would give her. Her desire was so sharp and strong that she had stumbled on her run, settling into a walk until the tightness between her legs relaxed and she could remember where she was and what she was doing and that she'd let Charlie go so she wouldn't hurt her.

Now, having been face-to-face with the clear sadness Charlie felt, Elizabeth's dedication to the cause wavered, and she was glad to be meeting up with Carmen for happy hour before facing her empty apartment. They sat across from each other in a corner booth away from the bar, where people were stacked up three deep and well into celebrating the weekend despite the early hour. Carmen pulled a dark cherry from her Manhattan, slid it from its wood stake, and chewed on it while brushing some stray hair away from her face. It had grown out a bit over the last couple months and fell softly around her ears in a very becoming way. She wore a suit today, which was unusual but meant she had meetings instead of lab work, which she hated. It was no secret that she would despise the way Elizabeth spent most of her days—not that Elizabeth was in love with it herself, which was certainly part of the draw of continuing to do hands-on work.

Besides the suit, something looked different about her. They'd both dropped a few pounds with their shared dedication to marathon training, but this was something else.

Elizabeth said, "You seem…really happy. And you're never happy when you're dressed up."

Carmen grinned like the cat that ate the canary and looked college-age again. "I have a date. One I actually want to go on." He was part of the group that invested in Carmen's research, and she'd been "trying not to pine" after him since they'd met in the spring, but he'd asked her to dinner after their meeting today.

She said, "It was kind of adorable. He asked and then got flustered when he tried to clarify that he meant it as a date and not some work thing, but he clearly didn't want to say date."

Elizabeth was truly excited for her friend and asked every question she could think of about this (terrific sounding) guy, but seeing Charlie had thrown salt in the wound of their breakup, and Carmen eventually noticed that maybe Elizabeth's heart wasn't fully in this celebration and asked what was going on. Elizabeth told her about running into Charlie at her office building and her rumbling regret.

"You're doing the right thing for both of you," Carmen said.

"I'm not sure why I didn't do it better, but every time I tried to write or call, the words all seemed wrong with no real logic to them, too open to argument, and I was sure Charlie *would* argue, and I'd succumb, and nothing would change when literally everything needs to change."

"I think 'everything' is overstating it a bit."

"Well, it's not far off. I insist on equality at the office, but I lived my life like I was going to somehow land a wife, some little woman who would make my work-blighted days better by cooking me good food and turning my apartment into a home. I mean, I didn't think she would sit around and do nothing while I wasn't there, but I acted like it was someone else's duty to fill in the actual life part of my life."

"Actually, I think you truly imagined yourself alone."

Elizabeth sipped a vodka and tonic, savoring this one drink she was going to allow herself in the face of her run the next morning. The half-marathon distance felt intimidating, but Charlie would remind her that it was only a mile longer than the last long run she'd done the week before. Charlie, again. She sighed. "Or I made a point of not imagining anything at all. But if I'm going to be with someone and not end up twice-divorced like Sharon, don't you think I should bring something to the relationship other than a good salary, a low monthly mortgage, and decent fashion sense? Like, I don't know, some emotional intelligence? An impressive dish or two I could trot out on date nights? An interest in conversation that doesn't involve technology or business or a harangue about the endless array of stupid men I have to deal with all the time?"

"Lizzie, I think you're being a little hard on yourself."

"I want to wash dishes while she dries. Or dry while she washes. A partnership."

"I get your drift, believe me, and it makes me really happy to hear you say that, but maybe just focus on one thing at a time. Work a little less on a regular basis before you sign yourself up for a knife skills class at The Chopping Block. You've been who you are for a long time, and if you try to change everything overnight, you'll end up snapping back into old habits in a permanent way."

"Yeah, but Charlie—"

Carmen took Elizabeth's hand and squeezed it a shade too hard. "Let me tell you something. Remember how I was after the divorce? I was a wreck. Just miserable. Even though I knew it was the right thing, and my relationship with Nick had gotten so bad at the end, I kept thinking through it, wondering if I'd done this one thing different or he'd changed his mind about that other thing…and maybe my marriage would have been saved if this or that—or this *and* that. But maybe isn't life. It's not real. Change is hard and slow, much more like my science than your career. If you really want to turn a corner, you need to focus on yourself for a while and figure out what you really want outside of anyone else. That means you have to forget about Charlie. And hope for her sake that she forgets about you."

But Elizabeth didn't want to forget. Not yet. Maybe not ever.

CHAPTER ELEVEN

Twenty Miles

The weeks peeled off the calendar in the haze of a hot and humid summer. August erupted in week-long heat waves capped off with howling thunderstorms. Pounding rain and gusty winds were followed by brief respites that turned into yet another stretch of days when temperature and humidity both tested bearable limits. As their runs got longer, Charlie schooled her group on hydration and electrolyte intake, and their walking breaks changed to align with stops for water or Gatorade from paper cups lined up on folding tables that RRiotWear and other area stores and running groups manned along the lakefront path. Charlie stripped down to just a sports bra and shorts and spent quite a bit of time resembling a container of Neapolitan ice cream: layers of tan interrupted by the white shadow of her clothes and topped with a hint of sunburned pink on her shoulders and chest.

She fell off the wagon of stability into another depression: a few wobbly weeks where she felt both heavy with fatigue and flayed wide open, a raw sore that anything and everything set to throbbing. She couldn't keep her thoughts from Elizabeth, kept digging at the emptiness there like a tongue playing at the socket where a lost tooth had been. When she couldn't sleep, she ached to call Elizabeth and tell her she was in trouble, tell her she needed something to distract her from herself, needed to stand in Elizabeth's beautiful kitchen and pan-sear some scallops, blend up a sauce, watch Elizabeth close her eyes at the flavors Charlie had put together and hum in appreciation.

She had more encounters where her tongue-tied chagrin had led shop clerks, fellow commuters, and, once, a very attractive barista to think she was a cold bitch, and she refused to take most calls from her mom. Loneliness wasn't a new thing in her depression, but it had always been complicated and contradictory, where she hated the enormity of her solitude but bristled at the thought of someone getting too close. But Elizabeth broke the mold of her habitual thoughts, and calling her or fantasizing about being held, still and quiet, was incredibly hard to resist.

She refrained, barely. She also stayed away from her couch and pajamas and *Law & Order* reruns. She forced herself to eat salads and take vitamins and go running and lift weights as if it wasn't torture to operate at odds to her desire to climb into bed and abdicate everything. She stayed out of her apartment entirely, reading her textbooks and writing papers at The Coffee Studio on the evenings she didn't drag herself to class. She saw Dr. Chatterbee, who agreed that she could try to ride it out for a while before changing her dosage—or maybe adding another drug into the mix to fine-tune.

"You're doing everything right," he said, so she wondered why it felt like everything was wrong.

At night, she huddled in her bedroom with her window air conditioner and stared at the ceiling through its rattling hum, willing herself to wake up to a morning free of humidity and paralyzing sadness. And one morning, she did. August had tipped into September during her doldrums, and the city had finally gotten the hint that maybe fall was coming. Charlie emerged from her bedroom buzzing with a mellow kind of energy that wasn't mania but *was* delicious. Her legs were strong and her lungs felt clear, and she pulled on her favorite long-run shorts, slipped into a pair of seamless, blister-busting socks, and opened a window to feel a breeze that couldn't quite be called cool but felt like a benediction anyway. A sleeveless running top protected her shoulders, which still hosted a few peeling edges of dead skin from her last sunburn.

She was early, so she buzzed the sides and back of her head over the sink and rinsed off tiny, itchy hairs under the faucet, which required her to bend over almost double. She pushed her wet hair back and under a white running cap, strapped on her watch, and headed out the door. She would take her group of four remaining runners—Jamie and Julie, who had clearly become good friends; Tamara, who had shed most of her baby weight; and Wendy, who'd kept running after her late-summer wedding and could join a faster group by now if she wanted—south all the way past the 31st Street Beach and then back north, blowing by their meeting place and up to Montrose, where RRiotWear was having their second party of the training season.

There would be food and merchandise and music and even a couple of massage therapists around to work on runners' legs, pushing the byproducts of their effort out of their muscles and fresh blood in to speed up healing. Pretty much the entire RRiotWear staff would be there, manning tables and happily swiping credit cards. Some of them would be there even now, setting up while the three training groups put in their miles with their respective RRiotWear leader. Amber had given Charlie free rein in expanding on their earlier party, creating an event webpage and related advertising, selecting the inventory to have on hand, and cross-pollinating with other running clubs. Through the remnants of her disappointment about not being who Jennifer and Veronica had wanted for this position, Charlie could admit that Amber was a decent boss and not out to take credit for Charlie's ideas. Still, this party had to go well, or it would reflect poorly on Charlie's abilities, but in this beautiful, temperate morning, Charlie couldn't work up any real worry, which was a wonderful thing.

The lake was a startling blue, and her group was milling around, looking equally excited and nervous about the twenty miles ahead of them. "Your legs know what to do at this point. If you don't go out too fast, which you won't with me around, you'll be fine. You'd be fine for even several more miles, so be happy you *only* have to do twenty today. Ready, set, go!"

Maybe, Charlie thought, she was actually a little happy, and not just because she was, at the moment, free of the clinging depression she'd fought for weeks. She was proud of this upcoming party, proud of these four women for sticking with her and improving week after week. She was proud of the course she'd managed to work her way through at Northeastern, and the bigger one about capitalism and government that had started the week before. Though she didn't want to leave RRiotWear, she'd been considering sprucing up her résumé (or actually putting one together) and seeing if she got any nibbles—even without a college degree, which would take another couple years unless she started doubling up on her course load. It felt almost as if spring was coming after a dreary winter instead of the opposite, but maybe it was just that she was finally waking up after the long slumber of her twenties.

Either way, she rode this wave of well-being through the miles, letting her legs carry her over asphalt and concrete, chatting up one member of her group or the next or giving them space to work through low points and quiet times. She'd made athletics into a strict hobby after the disaster of college, afraid of what competition would do to her brain chemistry if she tried it again, but coaching these women through this thing that was still new and hard and daunting made her wonder if she should get out from behind a desk entirely, stop trying to conform to corporate expectations (even those as minor and nebulous as RRiotWear's) and do something like this full time.

She knew something about motivation, about habits, about knowing when to push and knowing when to ask for help. She knew about commitment and listening to your body and plenty of delicious ways to avoid eating junk food without feeling deprived. She coasted into Montrose Park on the rolling threads of possibility and was stunned at the throng that had gathered. Veronica jogged toward her, yelling from ten feet away, "Holy shit, Charlie. You did it."

Charlie slowed to a stop. "As long as they're buying."

"Oh, they're buying. We're going to run out of inventory, I'm sure, so those tablets were a great idea. Order online while they're thinking about it and with just a little bit of hand-holding. I bet Amber used to work at a clothing store in college with the way she's selling the merchandise, tablet in hand and superlatives out the wazoo."

"Out the wazoo?"

"Cut me a break. I haven't eaten yet. Speaking of, come on." She pulled at Charlie's arm until they were loping to the food area, starting with orange slices and moving on to Chicago-style hot dogs and Mrs. Fields cookies. With the lifting of her depression and the twenty miles she'd just run—not including the two from her apartment to the totem pole—she wanted to eat everything in sight but limited herself to a couple hot dogs. She was halfway through the second one when she noticed Carmen at the cookie table not five feet away.

She couldn't stop herself from drifting a couple steps closer and saying, "Hey."

"Oh, hi."

Though she didn't want to, she kept her tone light. "Today was a relief, huh?" She motioned around them. "The weather, I mean."

"Yeah, though I'd kill for it to be twenty degrees cooler. I was definitely wilting toward the end."

"I can't disagree. I'm a dedicated winter runner, so it's been a challenging summer." She took another bite of hot dog to stop her own inane chatter—and to keep from asking what she'd come over here to ask.

Jessica appeared while Charlie's mouth was full. "Nice job putting this together, Chuck. I coerced most of the dykes in Frontrunners to show up. Hey, Carmen," she said, making it sound like an afterthought.

"Jess."

"I'm somehow not at all surprised that Elizabeth's missing. How long did it take for her to let her job consume her training?"

Carmen rolled her eyes. "Actually, she's doing her miles solo today. We're meeting up later when she's done."

The hot dog turned to paste in Charlie's mouth, and she looked around for some water to help wash it down but refused to move away from these two women.

Jessica arched an eyebrow. "Really. I'm…Really?"

"She's cut back a lot at the office. I think she's trying to reinvent her role there, but she's being tight-lipped about it."

"Are you sure we're talking about the same Elizabeth?"

"Yea high, brunette hair, MIT grad?" Carmen held her hand out just above the level of Charlie's shoulder.

"That's the one. Well, good for her, I guess." Jessica tilted her head at Charlie, who was still forcing down the last of her hot dog, and said, "See ya, Chuck."

Charlie said, "Don't forget to do some shopping."

Jessica waved at her over her shoulder.

Charlie and Carmen looked at each other. Charlie said, "I'm…glad she's still running. It seemed like she was starting to like it before we…before she…well, just before."

"She's committed, at least. She's the best person I know at seeing things through—once she decides to do it. Until then, she can be incredibly stubborn at not doing anything at all. You'd think that being rolled out of your office on a stretcher and taken by ambulance to the ER for a heart attack scare would prompt a thorough reevaluation of your unhealthy attitude toward work, but it still took months." Carmen had mostly been talking to the table of cookies and the lake beyond it, but she suddenly seemed to realize everything she'd just said and looked at Charlie, her eyes wide.

"She went to the hospital?"

"Before she started running. And it was just a panic attack. But she really wouldn't want me to tell anyone."

"Why didn't she tell *me*?"

"Charlie, listen. Apparently she didn't handle things with you very well, but it turned out the way it needed to. Or at least the way it would have, anyway."

"Why do you say that?"

"It's not worth going into."

Charlie crossed her arms. They were tacky with drying sweat. "Is this because I didn't go to MIT like you guys? Because I'm, what, intellectually inferior? Because I'm a jock?"

"Hey, I'm not the one who broke up with you, and it's not like I agree with how Elizabeth operates."

"And how does Elizabeth operate?"

"She lives in fear of boredom, which isn't really boredom at all but the unknown of what will happen if she shifts her brain from overdrive into neutral. Or not even neutral but…normal. She's incredibly frustrating that way. Her job is like this holy grail to her, the thing that keeps her moving forward, probably because she has no idea what to do with herself when she's not working on the next big thing. She's exhausting, I think to herself too, not that she would admit it, but she's her own person. In her mind, only someone who pushes her on an intellectual level could ever lure her away from the kind of constant stimulation her work gives to her, so if you don't challenge her mind, you're gone. Eventually. I've seen it multiple times, and it's never pretty."

"Just because I didn't go to an Ivy League school doesn't mean I'm stupid."

Carmen closed her eyes in a wince. "You're not stupid."

"I *know* I'm not stupid. That's exactly what I just said." Charlie's voice was too strident, which made her sound defensive. A few people swiveled to look at them but turned quickly away. "Sorry," she mumbled.

"I never said I agreed with her, but I know her. I've known her for twenty years, and I told her she shouldn't lead you on just to stomp on you later. Why do you think Jessica's so bitchy about her? Their breakup was *not* fun, even as a spectator."

"You convinced her to dump me?"

Carmen's face twisted in a grimace. "That sounds…not like what I was trying to do. It was for your own good. I could see the writing on the wall. She didn't want to."

Charlie laughed, but it felt like glass in her throat. "This just keeps getting better."

"You're making it into something it's not."

"Where's she running today?"

Carmen reached out and put her hand on Charlie's arm. "I'm telling you, she's not a good bet. I may have suggested that she take your feelings into account, but she makes her own decisions, for better or worse, and she doesn't want to see you."

Those words turned her hot dogs into a brick in her stomach, and she walked away from Carmen. She wanted to transport herself back to her apartment, drown herself in her shower, and hide out until the sting of Carmen's bald truth dialed back from deadly to something she might, one day, be able to shrug off— one day when she had her degree and a business card and some objective respect she could wear as armor against other people's judgment of her. But this was her event, and she had to paste a smile on her face and pretend to enjoy it, mingle with customers and co-workers alike.

The thought of Elizabeth riding in a gurney out the glass doors of her office building, scared and in pain, twisted her gut. Why hadn't Elizabeth told her? Was it the same reason Charlie hadn't let Elizabeth in on her own struggles? What might have happened if they had been honest with each other? According to Carmen, it was too late (or too dangerous to poor, stupid Charlie) to find out. But was it?

Elizabeth was most definitely her own woman, but so was Charlie. She'd bucked convention with her dress and hair and even name. She managed her disease in her own, specific way— to her mom's constant chagrin. But she'd also sat back and let life pass her by, not just by shying away from going after what she wanted but by trying not to even want in the first place. Wanting was huge and dangerous because it could lead to practically anything. Charlie knew all about disappointment, but what if she actually got what she wanted and it was something bigger and more important than the just-right, gooey cinnamon roll after a long, hard run? The only thing worse than wanting something and not getting it was having something and losing it.

She was not her father, but even her father, as difficult a time as he'd had, had been able to fall in love with her mom and had cared about Charlie to distraction. Charlie wouldn't exist if he hadn't put himself out there and taken what he wanted, and the love in their family wasn't what had done him in; that was his own brain chemistry. Charlie had been fearless before everything had fallen apart in college. That Charlie would have shaken Carmen until she divulged Elizabeth's whereabouts and pit herself against Elizabeth's sky-high expectations without a second thought.

Was that Charlie really gone? Was the only part of her left the one that believed what Carmen was saying? No, Carmen didn't actually say she was stupid, but she said Charlie wasn't enough. That Elizabeth wouldn't think she was enough. That they, like Charlie's mom, were making decisions that they thought were the best for her without her knowledge or consent. Being coddled like this infuriated her, and this time she swore to herself she'd do something about it instead of just admitting defeat and hoping that it wouldn't send her reeling.

* * *

The Monday after her twenty-mile run, Elizabeth's legs held a sweet ache when she walked down the hall to the all-company meeting she'd called. The novelty of her body having transformed from this thing that existed merely to hold her head up into its own independent entity, full of needs and a complex web of pleasure, pain, strength, and weakness, was continually astounding. She'd dropped several of the extra pounds she'd been carrying around and actually found herself craving fresh vegetables. She'd re-created Charlie's salmon salad almost weekly, partly to remind herself of being cared for so expertly and partly because it was so damn delicious.

She honestly hadn't believed she'd be able to run this far *ever*, but running that far had made thoughts of Charlie cling to her, especially because she was well aware the second RRiotWear picnic had just gone down. Charlie would be over her by now, especially with how poorly Elizabeth had handled things between them. But hadn't that been part of the point? If she was going to spare Charlie's feelings, she had to make a clean break, turn Charlie against her in a way that the rejection would only hurt temporarily and soon feel like dodging a bullet.

Weren't they both dodging bullets? When she lay in bed at night, Elizabeth could now feel the solid evenness of her pulse, and she hadn't had a panic attack in weeks, but she wasn't quite done with her transformation. All of this: the running, cooking, Carmen's admonishments, the sacrifices she'd made—not just giving up Charlie but giving up almost everything—had to come to something, didn't they? Despite her problem-solving skills, the *what* she'd been working toward eluded her. Her long runs since leaving the protection of the group (and the comfort of Charlie) had included as much thinking as exercise; large, existential questions that seemed both the perfect accompaniment to her lakeside jaunts and the absolute worst things she could ponder when all the oxygen in her body was feeding her legs instead of her brain.

Carmen had called the problem of her life too big to tackle all at once, and she'd been right. Just like running twenty miles happened step-by-step—or at least in five very familiar four-mile increments, she'd had to take it piece by piece. How do you eat an elephant? One bite at a time. Until now, though she didn't have everything worked out, she had a direction forward. Still alone, but having it all was a myth.

The conference room was jammed, standing room only—and not much at that. She squeezed past people with a smile to get to the front of the room, where they'd left a chair for her. Instead of sitting, she stood behind it with her hands on its back.

Dennis reached a connector out to her that she would usually use to project her laptop onto the monitor behind her, but she waved it off.

Everyone watched her, even more listening on the conference call piped through a squat speaker in the middle of the table. She had a sudden urge to not say what she was going to say, put into motion the plan she'd devised and had worked through with Dennis and Tyler over the last couple weeks, but she took a deep, grounding breath and dove in. "You all know how much I hate meetings so you are probably wondering why I'm making literally everyone attend this one. First, let me assuage any fears you might have: No, we're not in trouble. No, I'm not selling the firm. And no, I'm not changing our direction or approach or offices. I'm actually looking to change *myself* a little bit. I know, I know. 'Elizabeth, don't change; you're perfect the way you are. We love you.'"

The words and variation in her tone brought about the expected laughs, and she let herself chuckle a little along with them. But then she sobered and said, "I'm going to step back from a lot of the day-to-day operation and execution of our existing, mature offerings. To keep the ship running smoothly, I'm promoting Dennis to be our new Chief Operating Officer. It's well deserved, and he's going to be great." She started a round of applause that everyone seemed to join wholeheartedly.

"Now, don't worry. I'm not going to be a freeloader. I'm here to help Dennis and will be involved in servicing our largest and most strategic clients, but I'm changing my focus to be primarily on emerging technologies. What's just after this bleeding edge we've been dancing along for the last five years? How can we leverage new concepts to serve our customers and the industry? Because I want us not only to stay relevant but to become indispensable. I want other technology leaders to be looking to us for crafting the best practices for things other consulting firms don't even see coming yet. We're going to be the advance team, and I'm committing to lead that charge. Sound exciting?"

Heads around the room bobbed, and there were some quiet whoops and claps. "I'm going to be forming a small group within the firm where people will spend half their time on billable work and the other half collaborating directly with me to map out the future. But before that, I'm taking a two-month sabbatical to do some research and planning to better define this group's mission. I'll be back to present a more detailed vision and start interviewing for the positions I think will serve the mission the best.

"So, if you don't see me around for a while, imagine me in mad-scientist mode, researching and having my mind blown on a daily basis. And know that I can only do this because of what a great team we have here and our incredible level of professionalism and personal accountability."

They talked through details of Dennis's transition and some ideas of what she was thinking about for beyond the bleeding edge, and when she left the conference room almost an hour later, she was both exhausted and buzzed. She glanced around her office, which she might not see for a while if she managed to stick to her plan. Almost everything she really needed was available remotely: her books were digital, her files were in the cloud, she didn't even have a physical phone here. She slipped her two laptops and their power cords in her bag and added her favorite mouse. She ducked behind her desk and dug around for the stash of notebooks she kept in the bottom drawer, and when she stood up, Charlie was hovering in her doorway.

"Oh." A blurt of surprise erupted from Elizabeth. "I—Hi. What...?"

"I saw Carmen at the picnic over the weekend. I tried not to come here...but not very hard, I guess."

Charlie's hands were in the pockets of brown slacks with a soft windowpane pattern, and her dark blue shirt was turned up at the cuffs. She looked tan and healthy and heart-stoppingly handsome. And somehow beautiful at the same time. Elizabeth said, "It's good to see you." The understatement of the century.

"Carmen said you didn't want to see me."

Only because she wanted to see Charlie too much.

"She said you made up your own mind about things and would inevitably dump me."

"I was just—"

"She told me about your panic attacks."

Anger and relief collided in her, and she glanced through the glass walls of her office to see if anyone had been around to hear that. "Carmen should've stayed out of this."

But Charlie kept talking. "I wanted to tell you that I'm bipolar. The kind where you mostly get depressed, but the depression is episodic. It could last a couple days or a few months. I never know," Charlie said. "When we met, it was a struggle for me to get out of bed, which makes me…less than approachable. It started in college, which I went to but didn't finish because I drank too much and popped pills like candy since I hadn't found the right medication to make me stable." She spoke in a normal voice, as if stating dispassionate facts, but she looked right into Elizabeth's eyes. A humming connection made it impossible for Elizabeth to glance away, and her heart sped up—not like her panic attacks but almost like she was running, the beats strong and rhythmic and unstoppable.

"I don't know what to say," she admitted.

"I don't like when people make decisions for me, when they treat me with kid gloves or dismiss me because of my lack of degree or my mental illness."

"I wasn't—I didn't even know any of that."

"But you don't think I'm smart enough for you."

"Did you come here just to attack me?"

Charlie frowned and ducked her head. "You stopped us right when we were getting started."

Elizabeth wanted to vault her desk and launch herself across the room at Charlie. She wanted to wrap her arms around her strong torso and bury her face at the base of her neck, where it met her chest. "I'm not good at relationships, and I—"

"So you don't even want to try? You weren't good at running before we met, and yet you ran twenty miles over the weekend."

Elizabeth looked out the window. She'd run those miles because of Charlie, had run them *for* Charlie, even though she thought Charlie would never know. She dragged her gaze back to Charlie and waited for her to look up. Then she said the truest thing she could manage. "I couldn't live with myself if I really hurt you."

"I'm not a machine like your laptop. You can't control how I feel or what might happen. If there's one thing my illness has taught me, it's that there are no guarantees. This might blow up spectacularly. But what if it doesn't? Or even if it does, do you want to miss out on all the good stuff that could come before the end?"

Thump, thump, thump. Elizabeth felt her heart in her head, but what powered it was excitement and desire rather than panic. She slung her bag over her shoulder, eased around her desk, and strode to Charlie. She hooked two fingers in the vee of Charlie's shirt below her unbuttoned collar and tugged until Charlie leaned down to her and they were kissing.

Oh, God. Her lips were so soft, and Elizabeth melted into them, into the warm huff of Charlie's breath she felt against her cheek. Their kiss was a fission of comfort and arousal, and Elizabeth pulled back before it could progress to a point where she might not be able to let Charlie go. She looked up at Charlie and said, "Take me home. To your place."

"Yours is closer."

"I want to see where you live."

"It's not much."

"It's yours, and that's all I need to know."

* * *

They took the Red Line to avoid rush-hour traffic on Lake Shore Drive, standing close together in the commuting crowd, close enough that Charlie could feel the heat of Elizabeth's body through the fabric of her slacks and the thin cotton of her shirt. They didn't talk because whatever they had to say to each other (which was a lot, suddenly) couldn't be said over the rattling of the train and the other half-shouted conversations going on around them. When they finally left the train and made their way down the two flights of stairs from the elevated platform, the late-summer air was soft, which made the quiet between them feel dense and still.

They walked west toward Charlie's apartment, close but not touching until Elizabeth reached out to take Charlie's hand and intertwine their fingers. "I'm taking a sabbatical," she said. "For the next two months, I'm stepping back from day-to-day work to figure out where we're going next. Maybe even just to remember how to think at that level, at a slower pace, toward a more distant destination. Carmen's been telling me to slow down for years."

"You know, most runners, especially beginning runners, always run too fast. They hover in this area between aerobic and anaerobic and don't get the benefit of either. Sometimes you need to slow down to ultimately go faster."

"Sometimes you do your best thinking when you're not thinking at all."

Charlie smiled. "I like that." After a beat, she said, "I'm taking classes at Northeastern to finish my degree. I've…" She scanned the tops of the brick buildings that lined the street they were walking down, suddenly nervous. "I've been really careful with myself for a long time. Things just went so horribly wrong in college, and I haven't wanted to let that happen again, but I've missed out on so much. I let myself be ruled by my mom's fears for me." She swallowed and felt her throat stick together. Then she told Elizabeth about her dad, about how it felt to lose control of your mind, or how exhausting it sometimes was to exert control, to try to change the course of rogue neurons.

Elizabeth squeezed her hand at intervals, which helped ground Charlie and make these revelations feel less like being flayed open for the whole world to see. It felt right to expose her weaknesses to Elizabeth instead of trying to pretend that they didn't exist, that she had everything under control, that she was as strong as her legs all over and at every level. When she was done, Elizabeth told her about the pressure she'd been putting on herself for years and how it all felt more than a little desperate sometimes.

The closer they got to Charlie's apartment, the more intimate (and quieter) their conversation, and the more aware Charlie was of Elizabeth's hand in hers, the proximity of her body, the curve of her cheek, the fall of her hair, and the soft rounding of her breasts under her blouse. Strange how desire could come from being emotionally exposed, but here it was: the lurching drop of her gut and the thickening of her throat that no amount of clearing could dissipate.

By the time they got to the front door of her building, they'd both gone quiet, and Charlie could feel a flush rising from her chest up her neck past the collar of her shirt. She let them in and led Elizabeth up the flight of stairs to her apartment, where she fumbled with her keys before unlocking the dead bolt. She let Elizabeth in and closed the door behind them. When she turned back around, Elizabeth was wandering through her living room into her kitchen, and disappeared down the short hall to her bedroom and bathroom. Charlie followed her.

Elizabeth stood in the doorway of Charlie's bedroom, gazing around at the (thankfully) made bed, the short bookcase next to her dresser, the framed black-and-white photographs of Chicago hanging on the white walls. "I like it."

Charlie reached an arm around Elizabeth's waist and pulled her close. Then they were kissing. Again. Finally. It was deep and intense and, somehow, unhurried. Inevitable. Elizabeth's mouth was warm and sweet, her tongue insistent then shy. Charlie's desire went from a low-grade fever to a barely controlled forest fire that turned her body molten and vibrating with sensitivity, and she moaned with it.

Elizabeth pulled back. "Jesus," she said in a low voice. Her hands reached for the buttons of Charlie's shirt. "I thought about this so much. I tried not to, but I couldn't help it. I didn't want to help it."

"Me too." Charlie pushed the pearled buttons of Elizabeth's blouse through their small holes.

"You're the one who wanted to take things slow."

"I didn't mean *this* slow." Her fingers couldn't move fast enough. She ducked down and kissed Elizabeth's neck and shoulder and the soft tops of her breasts that peeked out above the lace of her bra while she worked on the last of the buttons.

She straightened up and made quick work of her own shirt, shrugging it off her shoulders. Elizabeth ran her hands from Charlie's collarbones down across her small but sensitive breasts to the waist of her slacks. "No bra," she said. "I was so frustrated last time." Charlie's nipples hardened in response to Elizabeth's fingers, and she reached forward to unclasp Elizabeth's bra and pull her close to feel her skin to skin, a connection that was electric and shocked Charlie out of the rest of her control.

They staggered back and fell onto the bed, kissing and touching and fumbling with belts and buttons and zippers until, finally, they were naked together, Elizabeth on top of Charlie, aggressive again in that surprising and delicious way, her newly strong thigh pressed up hard between Charlie's legs, sending shoots of pleasure through her body. She tried not to seem so eager, not to *feel* so eager, but her body overrode her mind, and she felt herself shift her hips against Elizabeth's leg for more.

They kissed while rocking together, one of Charlie's hands on Elizabeth's back and the other on her behind, holding her close. Elizabeth pushed her face into Charlie's neck and made a low groan. "You're so wet. I can feel it just like this." She grazed Charlie's skin with her teeth, which made Charlie's breath catch.

She hadn't fantasized about Elizabeth like this, but this far eclipsed whatever she'd conjured up in her imagination. Elizabeth's breasts pressed against her own, and her skin was silk under Charlie's fingers. "I want you," she said and pulled Elizabeth toward her so they could kiss again.

"Tell me," Elizabeth said, her breath warm against Charlie's ear. "Tell me how to touch you."

Charlie pushed up against Elizabeth's leg again, finding a rhythm she didn't want to stop but that wasn't nearly enough. She remembered Elizabeth's parallel parking, her desire to be an expert at everything she did. "I want you inside me," she whispered.

Elizabeth shuddered. She shifted just enough to fit her hand between them. Despite Charlie's instructions, Elizabeth explored first, dragging her finger through Charlie's wetness and circling her clit. Then again. And again. Charlie felt sweat rise on her skin, and her breathing stopped and started with each repetition. When Elizabeth finally pushed one finger, then two, inside Charlie, they both released a gush of breath. Charlie succumbed to the movement of Elizabeth's fingers, wanting the feeling of them together, of the curve and press of fingertips inside her, against her, reaching deeply. Then Elizabeth's thumb brushed her clit, and Charlie clenched in orgasm, crying out and clutching Elizabeth while she shuddered with a series of aftershocks.

Elizabeth's fingers were still inside her when Charlie opened her eyes. "I don't usually...not that quickly..."

"I loved it." Elizabeth kissed her and started to move her fingers again, which felt so good, but Charlie took her wrist, pulled her gently away, and turned the tables, pressing Elizabeth back into the bed.

"My turn." Charlie smothered Elizabeth's protests with kisses, not letting up until she felt Elizabeth start to succumb. She turned her attention to Elizabeth's breasts, which she'd fantasized about for months. She'd remembered the feel of those nipples under her tongue so well, the taste of her skin, the firm press of pliant flesh against her cheek and lips. She grazed each nipple with her teeth and sucked until Elizabeth started to writhe beneath her. Charlie was starving for this, desperate to consume Elizabeth in any way she could. She could lose herself in Elizabeth's breasts, and she would, later, when things between them weren't so urgent and new. She kissed her way back up to Elizabeth's neck but slid her hand down between Elizabeth's legs to feel her arousal, hot and thick. She couldn't swallow past her choking desire as she explored Elizabeth's swollen flesh. God, she felt so beautiful.

Elizabeth hummed and pressed up against her. "Feels so good." Her hand fluttered around Charlie's forearm and her wrist, and the whole thing was wonderful but somehow not quite enough.

"I want to taste you," Charlie whispered and felt Elizabeth nod and the movement of her hips grow more pronounced. Charlie bit the soft flesh under Elizabeth's jaw, then kissed down Elizabeth's stomach and across a hip until she found what she was wanting so desperately.

The flavor of her was deep and sharp, and her clit was hard against Charlie's tongue. She groaned when she circled her tongue around it once, then again, and felt Elizabeth's response, a push of her hips that said, "More." And more was exactly what Charlie wanted to give. One of her hands snaked under a thigh and over a hip to press on Elizabeth's belly while she slid a finger into Elizabeth's scalding wetness. Everything was heat and motion and slickness. Elizabeth's hips thrust under Charlie's ministrations, and one of Elizabeth's hands found Charlie's head, threading fingers through her hair over and over.

"Oh, God. Don't stop," Elizabeth whispered. "Don't stop," she repeated for a while until the words were replaced with breath, and Charlie felt tension build under her tongue and around her finger until she pushed inside Elizabeth more deeply and pressed her tongue harder against Elizabeth's clit. Elizabeth made a surprised sound and pulsed twice around Charlie, then again when Charlie moved her finger and tongue to draw out Elizabeth's orgasm as long as she could.

Charlie rested her head on Elizabeth's belly while they both caught their breath, one hand cupping Elizabeth's right breast. She felt the push and pull of Elizabeth's breathing, felt the play of fingers against the shorn back of her hair.

Elizabeth said, "Why are things so easy with you?"

"That's not a common sentiment."

"Those other women were crazy."

"No, *I'm* crazy."

Elizabeth tugged a little bit on Charlie's hair to urge her to finish the climb back up Elizabeth's body so they were face-to-face on Charlie's pillow. "I'm not afraid of what you told me."

Charlie closed her eyes. "It can get…challenging sometimes."

"Like training for a marathon?"

"I'm serious."

"If it makes you feel better, I'm going to screw this up. I'm going to get lost in work again. I'm going to forget to call or have to fly out at the last minute to save the day for a client."

Charlie opened her eyes and smiled. "That's incredibly comforting."

"But I want to try. I want to try hard."

"You're going to need to be patient."

"Like waiting all these weeks to be with you?"

"I'm pretty sure that was your fault."

"I'm pretty sure you're right," Elizabeth said and kissed Charlie again.

CHAPTER TWELVE

Marathon Day

The morning of the marathon dawned cool and overcast: perfect running weather. Charlie and Elizabeth had spent the night at Elizabeth's apartment since it was so close to the start and finish of the race. Elizabeth woke up an hour before she had to and couldn't fall back to sleep but spent the time watching Charlie. Her shock of blond hair was wild on the pillow, the curve of her ear naked against the shorn hair at the side of her head. Charlie slept with abandon, breathing deeply (and sometimes noisily) in dreams, reaching for Elizabeth even when she wasn't nearly awake.

They'd spent the last month getting to know each other: eating plates of scrambled eggs and cheese in bed at the midnight's end to long lovemaking sessions, studying and working next to each other at 3 Greens several evenings, having brunch with Carmen and her new boyfriend after the last long run before today's race. Elizabeth had hunkered down in Charlie's apartment, working from her deep, plush couch in a persistent patch of sunshine that swept across her during the progression of each day, taking breaks to examine Charlie's things: the army of shirts and slacks in her closet that smelled like her, the shelves of books, a pile of soccer cleats and running shoes, a drawer full of kitchen implements, some of which had purposes that eluded her.

Charlie apologized for the size and shabbiness of the place, but Elizabeth loved it. It felt wonderfully lived-in, functional in a most comfortable way unlike the relative coldness of her own apartment. Besides, she loved being there when Charlie got home from work, flushed from the walk from the train and smiling with ready kisses and a desire for her that seemed unquenchable. Elizabeth delighted in their lovemaking. Charlie was so responsive and so willing to abandon herself to Elizabeth's touch...at least until she turned the tables and got deliciously bossy, lavishing attention on Elizabeth's breasts and neck and hips until Elizabeth was more than happy to succumb, losing herself in Charlie's smile and her fingers and her murmured commentary about what she was doing and what she planned on doing next—to which Elizabeth could only say, "Yes."

Sometimes she could sense an undercurrent of desperation in Charlie's desire, something beyond the exciting newness of it all that made hours apart feel untenable. It was as if she was frantic to get it all in *right now*, as much as possible. When Elizabeth would slow them down, Charlie would apologize and flush with an adorable embarrassment. But then her face would tighten with resolve, and she would be clear, once more, that when she got depressed again (she always said *when*, not if), this desire would surely evaporate—temporarily, she hoped. They both hoped.

But wasn't that what this whole thing was about? Hope? That the good would outweigh the bad? That the connection between them didn't need the façade of common careers or hobbies but could rest on this foundation of care and communication, of deliberateness and the plain recognition of each other's failings and challenges and strengths and desires?

Charlie breathed in a short breath then a long one and blinked awake. Elizabeth could see her pupils in the chocolate brown of her eyes constrict against the bedroom's relative brightness. She smiled. "Hey." Her voice was husky with sleep.

Emotion clogged Elizabeth's throat.

Charlie propped herself on an elbow and pushed some of Elizabeth's hair from her face. "Hey," she said again, but her voice was edged with concern. "What's going on? Are you nervous?"

"Yes, but not about the race." She captured Charlie's hand and kissed its palm. "I'm nervous because I'm falling in love with you."

"Don't." Charlie tried to pull her hand away, but Elizabeth held tight. "You can't say that until you've seen me—"

"We both have things about ourselves we're afraid will drive the other one away, but doesn't everyone? It's all part of you, and it's all part of me. We wouldn't be who we are if it weren't for what we've been through and done. And it's you that I love, this kernel of you indivisible from your sadness and excitement and love for the physical. I know what I'm getting into, and I'm nervous because of how much I want it."

"I want it too." Her mouth curled up in that half smile Elizabeth loved so much. Yes, loved. "I haven't wanted to try for anything that might fail in a long time, but I want to. For you." She kissed Elizabeth almost chastely. "This last month has been magical, but I want something more like this race today. Real and grounded with ebbs and flows and effort and those little notches of success each mile. Wanna run twenty-six miles with me and make it real?"

"Absolutely." They kissed again before Charlie rolled across the bed and to her feet.

Elizabeth watched her shuffle to the bathroom, pulling up drooping shorts while she went. The fact that Charlie hadn't said those three stupid, wonderful, important, useless, vital words back to her somehow didn't bother her at all. She would be patient. She would wait and see whatever Charlie didn't want her to see. She'd slow down, and Charlie would speed up, and they would be matched in the perfect middle, taking down miles and years, scary and hard and thrilling and victorious.

Elizabeth couldn't wait to get started.

Bella Books, Inc.

Women. Books. Even Better Together.

P.O. Box 10543
Tallahassee, FL 32302

Phone: 800-729-4992
www.bellabooks.com